I took a long drag off of my cigarette. I watched as the cherry burned down close to the two fingers, I was holding the butt between. I anticipated the burn, but did nothing to stop it from happening. It's just a little test that I give myself to see if I am still capable of feeling anything. Once the heat hit my index finger, I savored it. I let myself enjoy the pain for a few moments before crushing the source out in the ashtray. I poured some beer on the redness, not worrying if any of the excess liquid went onto the carpet.

After using the can of Busch Light as a crude form of pain management, I took a drink. The can felt light, so I reached into the mini fridge to make sure the next beer was ready when I took the last sip of the one that I was holding. I've always hated waiting for the next beer. I very rarely keep any food in the mini fridge, just beer. I buy it by the thirty pack. I hardly ever run out that way.

A freshly opened beer always goes better with a freshly lit cigarette, so I lit another one. I smiled at the blister that was already forming from my last Marlboro Light. From the corner of my eye I saw the lines of cocaine that were still sitting on top of cd case next to a curled-up dollar bill. I was tempted to do another one, but decided I was already pretty wired and I would probably need to start thinking about getting some sleep soon. If I decided that that was the way I wanted the night to end. I could see the shadows behind the blinds. Just waiting.

It was 3:17 in the morning. I watched as the moon shone through the leaves of the weeping willow tree that was outside my window. I thought about going out onto the balcony to enjoy the breeze but it seemed like too much effort at the moment. The noise would probably have disturbed my guest. She seemed to be sleeping soundly on the air mattress in the corner of my little rented room. I couldn't remember her name.

Next to the cd case with the coke was a nine-millimeter hand gun. As I picked it up, I asked myself why I was grabbing it. What were my intentions? It just felt good to hold. The weight of it in my hand seemed to offset the weight that was resting on my soul.

I studied the girl sleeping on my bed. She was way out of my league. Here I was, a fifty-year-old man with a receding hairline, false teeth and a growing beer belly. She probably wasn't even thirty yet, and was stunningly beautiful. She had long straight brown hair. Her face had high cheekbones giving her a very exotic look. She had long legs and a lean, toned body. The ass that I was staring at was flawless. I looked at all of the little scars on her body. Some were newer than others. She must have been a cutter.

Even though I didn't really know who she was, I had been expecting her, or someone like her, for a very long time, most of my life. I knew who she was and why she had come up and sat next to me at the bar. I didn't think too much of it at the time, but while I was having sex with her, she whispered in my ear, "You're not even real. You don't belong here."

I thought about those words as I drank and smoked. She wasn't the first person that had said something similar to me, but nobody else had put it so bluntly. I think that it was something I had always known, but it had taken a half of a century to realize what it meant.

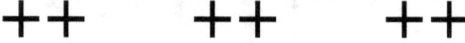

Maybe this girl in my bed was on to something. I never knew my parents, or even if I had any, and never really got an explanation of how I came to be in this universe. I was raised by a lady who was on the far end of being middle aged. She never really explained to me who she was or how I came to be in her care. I remember watching "The Addams Family" as a kid and she reminded me of Morticia, but older and not as funny. I would hear people say that she was my grandmother, but when I asked her, she would just ignore the question. We had minimal interaction throughout my childhood. She would do the basic things that a parent would do for a child, feed me, cloth me a keep a roof over my head, but she never played with me or taught me much. She seemed to have very little interest in me. Our relationship seemed to have a prisoner and guard dynamic rather than that of family.

I always called her Aunt Anima. She would call me Vitorum with a strange accent. Later in life, I guessed that it was eastern European. Everybody else called me Vincent. We lived in a rural farm house outside of Ordway, Colorado. Well, actually at one time it might have been a farm, but when I was a kid in the late sixties and early seventies the land was just a dry prairie of weeds. Every time there was a windstorm, there would be hundreds of tumble weeds smashed up against our front door.

On the opposite side of the small town was a state prison. It had a special section that was reserved for the criminally insane. That is where Anima worked. I never knew exactly what she did there, but I think that she was some type of nurse. I would never have described her as unkind, it just seemed that had no real interest in life. Her voice was always monotone, and the look on her face never seemed to change. She never laughed, but she never got angry either. It was like she was born without emotion.

Since there was very little conversation between Anima and me, I never considered asking about my mom or dad or whether I had any brothers or sisters. To be honest, it never really crossed my mind. I was educated at what was called a religious school that was on the same grounds as the prison, but there was never any religion that was taught that I remember. There were only a few other students at the school, but we weren't allowed to interact with each other. There were never recesses or gym classes. The subjects that were taught were just the basics, reading, writing and math. The whole experience was like being babysat by teachers who didn't like kids.

It wasn't until 1980 that I really even thought about my real family, that was the year that I got my driver's license. Anima handed me an envelope and told me that I would need to take it to the department of motor vehicles. Inside the envelope was my birth certificate. It turns out that my original name was "Baby Boy Johnston". The section for "father's name" was blank, and my mother's name had been covered by black magic marker. It was pretty obvious that I had been named by a doctor or nurse, or maybe I had just been left on Anima's doorstep.

She never told me why she called me Vitorum, and I don't remember how I came to answer to the name Vincent. Sometimes I wondered if I had just appeared out of thin air. The most vivid memory of my childhood was that at night, I could always see shadows moving across my bedroom wall when there was no light to create them.

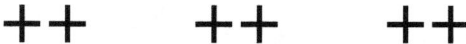

The night that I found I was born without a name was the first time that I had a singular type of dream that I would continue to have throughout the course of my life. I don't like to call them dreams, because that isn't really what they are at. They are too real. It feels like I am actually somewhere else. I refer to these dreams as "going to the Terminal."

The Terminal is a big building in the middle of nowhere. I could see out the windows that the building was in some type of valley. The foliage was all brown like it was on a prairie, but there were tall, jagged, treeless mountains surrounding the structure. I always figured if the place was real, it would be somewhere in the middle of Wyoming.

The reason I started calling it the "Terminal" was because it always felt like I was in a bus station or an airport. It was always a place that was filled with people going from one destination to another. You could never tell who was coming and who was going and you never saw where they went, they just faded out of sight. There was nothing significant that I can remember about the first time that I went there. People were just introducing themselves to me and saying "welcome".

I wasn't the only child that Aunt Anima took care of. I was the only one that was there for any length of time, but there were others that came and went. I know the reason for that had something to do with the people at the prison where Anima worked. They might have been the kids of the prisoners who now had nobody left to care for them. Some of the children were only there for a day or two, while there were others who stayed for weeks or even months. Most of them were young boys, but there were a few girls that passed through.

There was one little boy that was there longer than the others. His name was Xavier. He was a couple of years younger than me. He was the only one that ever left any kind of memory with me. He was always smiling and that puzzled me.

"Why are you always so happy?" I asked him once.

"I just am."

I remember his eyes very well. They seemed to be lit from the inside of his skull. All of the other kids that went through the house always seemed sad. Their eyes always looked like they were going to start crying at any time. Xavier was just different. In many ways he didn't even seem like a child.

Another thing that I always found odd about Xavier was that he had an extreme fascination with snakes. There were plenty of snakes around Ordway. You couldn't drive on the highway more than a mile or two without seeing a dead snake in the road. During summer vacations from school, Xavier and I would be home alone. Most of that time we spent on a limestone bluff, not too far away, so that he could look for snakes.

One day while we were on top of the cliff looking for snakes sunning themselves on ledges below, Xavier said, "Vincent look at my shadow." The sun was hitting him just right so that his shadow appeared to be that of a giant.

"What about it?"

"This is my time."

"Time for what?" I asked.

"I don't know. I just know that it is my time." Xavier started walking very fast on the path that took you to the bottom of the bluff and into a dense grove of trees. His pace quickened and I had trouble keeping up with him as I tried to navigate the thick brush.

"Wait for me," I yelled out to him. I had lost sight of him.

"I can't," he screamed back. "This is the biggest snake I have ever seen."

All I could do was follow in the direction that I thought he was going. I tried to run, but the foliage was just too thick. I started to hear something. It took me a while to realize that it was the sound of traffic. It kind of startled me because I never knew that there was a road even close to where we were. I looked up ahead and saw what appeared to be a clearing. As I approached it, I heard loud screech, then a deafening thud, then total silence.

After I got through the trees, I found myself on the shoulder of a two-lane black top. There was an old truck in the middle of the road. A tall dark shadowy figure stood in front of the truck. As I crept closer, I saw Xavier in the middle of the road. There was blood coming out of his ears and mouth.

"Vincent, run home and get Anima," the tall shadow told me.

I just stared at Xavier laying in the road. I didn't even look at the face of whoever it was that was speaking to me.

"Vincent, go get Anima," the voice said again.

As I turned to run in that direction, out of the corner of my eye I could see a rattle snake all coiled up on the other side of the road.

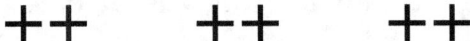

As I headed in the direction of the house, the initial panic that I had felt at seeing Xavier in the road for some reason completely disappeared. I felt no sense of urgency as I walked. Instead, I felt a sense of calm that I had never felt before. I had absolutely no worry about Xavier, even though I had no idea if he was alive or dead.

When I got back to the house and told Anima what had happened, she was stoic as always. She seemed to be just as calm about the situation as I was. She told me to go to my room and that she would be back soon. When she got back home, she didn't say a whole lot as usual, only that Xavier was going to be in the hospital for a very long time and that dinner would be ready soon.

The entire time that Xavier was in the hospital we never went to visit him. We didn't even speak of him. Anima never told me what was wrong with him or how badly he was hurt. He was just gone. It would be almost a year before I saw him again. I remember the day well; it was the day that I got my driver's license.

It wasn't too long after I got my driver's license in 1981 that I came home to find an old army jeep sitting in the driveway. I didn't think a whole lot about it, but I was surprised because there were very few visitors that actually drove out to the house. As I walked through the door, the first thing that I noticed was the stillness and silence. The place was empty. I called out for Aunt Anima or Xavier but there was no answer. I surveyed each of the rooms. There wasn't so much as a scrap of paper in any of them.

I saved the door to my room to be the last one that I checked. All of my furniture had been removed. There were two suitcases placed exactly in the middle of the room. On top of one of the suitcases was a set of keys. I picked them up. It was obvious that they were to the jeep that was parked out front. I opened the suitcases. They were filled with my clothes and the necessary toiletries. In one of the suitcases was a big envelope. It was filled with cash. I didn't count it, but I could tell it was a substantial amount because it was all twenties, fifties, and hundreds.

It didn't take me long to come to the conclusion that Anima was gone and that she had left no clue as to where she was going. I knew that I was probably never going to see her again and that was the way she wanted it. I didn't know what to think about Xavier. I doubted that she would have taken him with her, but I didn't think he left on his own either.

I loaded the suitcases into the back of the jeep, and climbed into the driver's seat. I sat there for a moment. I had no idea where I was going to go. The closest big road to the house was Highway 50, it ran east and west. When I got to it, I had to make a decision if I was going to turn left or right. I looked at the mountains in the distance and decided that I was going to head west. There really was no logic to the decision, it just seemed like the right thing to do.

The first real town that you come too heading west from Ordway is Pueblo. I had decided that I was going to camp along the way to wherever it was that I was going. I took some money out of the envelope and went into a K-Mart to get all of the supplies that I would need, like a tent, sleeping bag and food.

That old army jeep wasn't made for speed so the travel was slow. That didn't bother me because I didn't know where I was going anyway. After about a day and a half of driving, having passed over the Rocky Mountains, I found myself on a desolate desert highway driving towards Lake Powell in Utah. It was hot as fuck, at least a hundred degrees. The last town that I passed was eighty miles in the rearview mirror and I still had a good way to go before I got to the water. My plan was to camp there for a few days and think about just what it was that I was going to do with the rest of my life. Maybe I would just keep wandering.

Ahead, in the distance, I saw a figure walking on the side of the road. As I passed by, I saw that it was a guy who was maybe sixty, with a grey pony tail that almost stretched down to his ass. He was wearing a crumpled old leisure suit and red Chuck Taylor tennis shoes. He carried a small blue back pack like a kid would carry to school. The guy had his thumb out searching for a ride. At first, I passed him by, but something told me that he was somebody that I need to meet. I flipped a U-turn and went back to pick the old guy up.

"Where are you headed?" I asked him.

"Nowhere at the moment. I just have a gathering a few states away that I need to be at in two or three weeks."

"I'm heading to the lake for a few days. I have plenty of food. You are more than welcome to hang out with me until you need to start heading in the direction of where you're going."

He studied me for a while, then just nodded in agreement.

"What kind of gathering are you going too?"

"It's just a thing where people who all think the same way go," he said.

"What does that mean?"

"Unless you think the way that I do, I really couldn't explain it to you."

"My name is Vincent."

"I'm Miles. Nice to meet you. That was nice of you to pick me up." His face was weathered making him look older than I knew he was. He was in great physical shape for a man of his age.

"Where you from?"

He kind of chuckled. "Son, I've been on the road so goddamn long I don't really remember. I guess home is wherever I am at the moment."

In about an hour, we had a campsite set up on the beach of a serene cove on the lake. Red and orange cliffs towered over us in all directions. We built a campfire and I made a pot of rice and beans. He just stared up at the stars while he ate without saying a word. I could tell that he wasn't just looking at the stars, it was like he was looking for something specifically. He would get fixated on something in the sky then give a wry smile and shake his head.

About an hour after we had finished eating, the old man pulled a little tea kettle out of his backpack. He walked to the water's edge, put some water in it, then came back and put it on the fire. I was about to light a joint, but he told me I should wait a while before I smoked it.

"Why?"

He pulled a small sphere out of his backpack that was wrapped in foil. He took the foil off and put it into the tea kettle. "You should try this."

"I'm not a real big tea drinker," I said.

He ignored my protest and poured me some of the liquid into a rust tin cup.

"I don't like tea," I told him again.

"This isn't tea."

"What is it?"

"Ayahuasca."

"I've never heard of it."

"You need it."

"For what?"

"It will show where you're going."

I took a sip, it tasted fucking awful but I managed to tolerate the taste and finish the cup of liquid. It made me feel a little light headed at first, but after a while it made me feel like I didn't have a head at all. The sky above me just completely shattered and fell perfectly onto the tops of all of the cliffs that surrounded us. The pieces of the sky started to take the form of something humanly and they all walked right to the edge.

Through the shattered sky, the sun appeared out of nowhere and illuminated the figures on the top of the cliffs. My eyes felt like they were bowling balls rolling around in my eye sockets. I noticed that all of the figures, millions of them, all looked exactly the same. The all had the same face. It was a face that I recognized. It was my face, and they were just all there standing in silence and staring down at me.

I kept thinking about the old man as I stared at the girl sleeping naked on my air mattress. I glanced over at the cocaine on the cd case and decided that I didn't really need to go to sleep so I did another line. The sound of my snoring made my guest stir a little. I was about to say something but all she did was roll over.

When I saw her face, I tried hard to remember who she was. I had gone to the bar earlier that evening with no intention other than to get as shit-faced drunk as I possibly could. I was about half way to my desired destination when she sat down next me. She said hello to me and I responded likewise without really looking at her. I was content to just stare into my glass of beer. She kept trying to engage me with small talk and I went along with it, but no real words of consequence were exchanged.

It wasn't until she got up to go to the bathroom that I realized what a fantastic body she had. Once she returned, I was more open to a conversation with her. It wasn't that I really cared what she had to say. I had an ulterior motive. I really wanted to fuck her. It had been a long time since I had had sex. I had long since resigned myself to life of loneliness.

As she spoke, I realized that there was a deep sense of loneliness about her as well. I could tell by the look in her brown eyes that that night she didn't want to be alone. It would have been easy for me to dismiss her as just a typical barroom slut, but somehow, I knew that wasn't the case. She spoke very articulately. It was obvious that she had a form of higher education or she just liked to read a lot.

As the conversation at the bar slowly came back to me, the was one little exchange between us that stood out.

"What year were you born," she asked me.
"1965"
"What was your mom like?"
"I never knew her."
"Are you adopted?"
I told her that I wasn't really sure. It was never really explained to me.
For some reason that answer made her quiet. She looked at me pensively.
"Don't pity me," I said to her.
"Oh, I'm not. I was just thinking that if abortion had been legal in 1965 there is a good chance that you wouldn't be here right now".
"That's true, I guess."
"Do you think about it?
"Do I think about what?" I wasn't sure what she was getting at.
"That maybe you're not supposed to be here."

I didn't want to tell her that it was something that I thought about all the time, so I just said, "not really".

The morning after drinking the Ayahuasca with Miles, I woke up feeling like a completely different person. My whole body felt different. I felt heavier. My bones seemed to have a dull ache from head to toe. There seemed to be some kind of shroud covering me, but when I touched it, I realized that it was hair. I followed it up to my face. I had somehow grown a beard that had reached down to my knees. I looked over at Miles, who was packing what little he had into the backpack.

"What the fuck?" I asked. "How long was I out for?"

"How am I supposed to know?" he said. "There is no such thing as time. It's a manmade thing. The only reason there are clocks is so simpletons have some point of reference."

"Do you have a mirror?"

"Don't look in a mirror," Miles said. "It will only give you an illusion of you think you are".

He through the back pack over his shoulder and said goodbye.

"Why are you leaving so soon?" I asked him.

"I've experienced everything that I have needed to experience here, and now it's time for me to start moving again. There are people that will be expecting me soon."

"At the gathering?"

"Yes."

"Where is it?"

"It's somewhere in Montana. There are two Indian reservations up there, and it's somewhere between the two of them. I don't know how long it will take me to get there."

"Well, thank you," I said. "It was nice having your company."

"Good luck to you Vincent. I hope you find what you're looking for."

Despite what Miles had said to me, I grabbed a mirror from one of the suitcases in the jeep. I used it to look at myself. It seemed to me like I had gone from a teenager to a man in what seemed to be overnight. The beard in front was almost as long as my hair had grown from my head, and it was now on my chest too. I guessed that I was probably two or three inches taller and had gained at least 25 pounds.

I watched Miles walk down the dirt road that weaved through the cliffs until he was out of sight. I crawled back into my tent and just lay on the top of my sleeping bag. Even at that early hour, the sun was already scorching the Earth. I started to sweat profusely and thought about all of the millions of figures that had stared down at this brew of flesh and bones that I call a body from atop the cliffs the previous night. I had a feeling that they were trying to tell me something, but I wasn't listening. I remember seeing it their eyes.

I got out of the tent, stripped naked, and walked down into the lake. A strange feeling came over me. The water was perfect. It was cool enough to sooth the heat, but not so cold that it was a shock to the system. I floated on my back with my ears under water to silence what little noise there was anyway. I closed my eyes and made it so that only my nose and mouth weren't submerged. My body started to tingle. A calm stillness engulfed me. I thought about just letting myself slip under the water's surface forever, but this feeling I was having was like a drug. I felt lost and found at the same time.

In the stillness of being under water, I heard a voice say my name. The voice was calling out to me. I rushed out of the water, put on a pair of shorts and my sandals. I took a pair of scissors from the jeep, and cut most of the beard off, it was driving me crazy. I packed the campsite into the jeep as fast as I could and started driving in the direction that the old man had gone. He couldn't have gotten that far. I kept driving, but there was no sign of him. In the water, it occurred to me that I should be at the gathering he was heading to. There was no sign of Miles. I thought about turning around, but there was no way that I could have missed him. Maybe he decided to walk off of the road. The fastest way from one destination to the next is a straight line. I was disappointed, but that's just how life is sometimes.

I had pretty much resigned myself to the fact that, just like Anima, I was never going to see Miles again. Just as I thought that, I saw the old man walking on the road ahead of me. I stopped, "need a ride," I asked.

"Sure."

"Did you get a ride from someone else?" Miles had quizzical look on his face when I asked him that. "Did you take some kind of shortcut? I've been driving for two hours, there is no way that you could have walked this far in that amount of time."

He put his hand on my shoulder, "Vincent, time and distance aren't always what they appear to be."

"Can I give you a ride to the gathering?" I asked.

He got into the jeep and we started driving. "I thought about asking you if you wanted to go last night", he said. "I wasn't sure if you would fit in. That's why I left this morning. I figured that if you belonged there you would find me.

The only thing that Miles knew for certain was that it was somewhere in the mountains in northern Montana. It was between the Blackfeet and Flathead Indian reservations. It would probably take us two or three days to get there.

"You never did tell me where you were from," I said.

"I grew up in Santa Fe."

"Do you still have family there?"

"I don't have a family. My father was a crazy alcoholic. One night in June of 1967 he got drunk and shot my mother and then himself."

"Wow. No brothers or sisters?"

"No."

"What did you do?"

"I was seventeen, and for some reason joining the army seemed like a good idea. I spent the next two and a half years in Vietnam. When I got out of the service, I reckoned there was nothing for me back in Santa Fe, so I've been on the road ever since. What about you? What's your story?"

I told him about life in Ordway. I told him about Anima and Xavier and how they had just disappeared and that I had decided to take off. There wasn't a whole lot to tell. "What was Vietnam like?" I asked.

He stared at me hard. I could tell that it was a question that I should not have asked. "I don't like to talk about it," he finally said. "I did some very bad things over there. Some things that a human wouldn't do. That's why I stay on the road. There's nobody asking me about it."

"Sorry."

"It's okay."

We drove in silence for the next few hundred miles.

The don't exactly print maps to "the gathering of like minds" as Miles liked to call it. When we got close, he would tell me where to turn, but for the most part he was just guessing. A couple of times he had me stop the jeep so he could just get out and listen. When he got back in, he would tell me which way to drive. When we were going across a dirt mountain pass, he said that he thought we were very close. We passed a little road that Miles looked at very hard. At first, we passed the road by, but then he said that we needed to turn around and go down the road.

"Sometimes they camouflage the road. They don't want to attract the shadows. If you are like minded, you'll eventually find the place."

I wanted to ask him what he meant by "shadows" but decided not to. We kept on driving on that little road until we reached the summit of the mountain. Once we started our descent down the other side, we could see a big valley below us. There were probably a hundred tents set up over a two square mile area. There was a lake in the middle of the valley created by a river that flowed in from one side and out the other.

"Were here," Miles said.

As we drove into the valley, there were hundreds of people engaged in various activities. There were several campfires with people sitting around them drinking beer and getting high. There were people grilling food on barbecues. There were a few people swimming in the lake. Many of the people were walking around naked, and the ones that were wearing clothes were wearing very little. There were people having sex with each other. Men were having sex with women; women were having sex with other women and men were having sex with other men.

"Why are all these people like minded?" I asked Miles.

"That is something you will either figure out or you won't," he said as he started walking towards the trees.

"Where are you going?"

"I like to camp in the trees. The people are more interesting there. You camp wherever you want."

I set my tent up by the lake. I have never been the most social of people. Considering I was raised in a house by a woman who barely spoke to me, it's no surprise that I have never been comfortable walking up to total strangers and starting a conversation. For most of my life, I had wondered if I was invisible. With the old man up in the trees I spent my first couple of days there just observing the people around me. Some people invited me to eat with them, and others let me drink beer around the fire with them. I had no clue what made all of these people like minded.

On my third night there, I sat alone around my own little campfire smoking a joint. I was wondering how much longer I was going to say there. It didn't seem like I was fitting in. Everybody there seemed so strange to me. I had never seen the ocean before, and knew that I could get there in a couple of days. I had always wanted to see it. I didn't know whether I should search out Miles and tell him what I was thinking or not.

I was lost in thought and fixated on the flames in the circle of rocks in front of me when I heard a soft voice say "hello". I looked up to see a tall, sandy blond girl standing in front of me. She was wearing a bikini top and cutoff jean shorts. She had a beautiful smile and was maybe two or three years older than me. She had a few tattoos but I couldn't really make out what they were in the light of the fire.

"Hello," I said.

"I've been watching you since you got here. It doesn't seem like you have noticed me."

"I've seen you around. I just thought that you were with some other guy."

She laughed. "At these gatherings, no one person is with another person. Everybody is with everybody. That's why we're hear."

"I'm Vincent."

"My name is Diane. Do want to take a walk with me?"

"Sure."

She grabbed my hand and we started walking along the river. "I found a secret little place the other day."

"Are we going to be able to find it in the dark?"

"Don't worry," she said. "I've spent my entire life navigating the darkness. Besides, the moon is almost full, we'll be able to see."

We followed the river until we came to a shallow part of the river and walked across it. She pulled a plastic bag from her pocket and asked me if I wanted to eat some mushrooms. "Okay," I said.

"I have this friend who barely leaves his house. All he does is grow mushrooms. He doesn't really do them that often, and most of the time he will just give them away for free."

"That's cool, I guess. I don't understand why he would do that though."

"I asked him that once," she said. "He just said that he wanted as many people as possible to truly experience life to the fullest."

We split the contents of the bag and kept walking until we came to a waterfall.

"This is it," she said. "This is my favorite place."

"I can see why." There was a deep pool at the bottom of the falls. Off to the side of that was a grouping of rocks that seemed to form a natural hot tub. The mushrooms were really starting to kick in, we would both start laughing for no reason at all. Diane took off her bikini top and threw it at me. She took off her shorts and waded into the water.

"Aren't you coming?" She asked. I took off my shorts and followed her in. The liquid was surprisingly warm. We sat together on a rock that kept the water right at the level of our chests. She must have really been tripping hard because she started talking about her soul and its place in the universe and that she could go anywhere she wanted just by thinking about it. As she talked, I just stared up at the stars. I realized that I never really studied the stars before, the sky was spectacular. The mushrooms made me feel as though I wasn't just seeing the heavens. I was understanding them.

"The old man that I came here with told me that this gathering was for people who thought the same way. What way are thinking?"

"All of us," she said, "are trapped in an existence that we were never supposed to be in. This is one of the lower universes in an infinite number of universes. This place is for the souls that believe everything who believe everything they hear or read. The souls on this plane of existence are those that have a complete lack of ability for critical or logical thought."

I pulled her close to me and kissed her. "Do you ever feel lonely?" she whispered in my ear.

"I've felt it every single day of my life."

"I feel the same way. It's all I've ever known. Everybody here feels the same way. Souls are kindred by nature, that's how we all know how to find these places."

Her words made sense to me. I don't know if those words would have made sense to me if I had not eaten the mushrooms, but at that moment I completely understood everything that she was saying.

"We've found each other." As she said that, I was looking into her eyes. It was like I was seeing her for the first time.

"I know. I don't know how, but I know."

"Vincent, we've met a thousand times before, and we'll meet a thousand more times after this one."

I knew what she was saying. "Where have you been?"

"Everywhere."

I kissed her again, but this time it felt different. It was more than a kiss; it was some kind of connection. She wasn't just some girl I had met at a random gathering. I felt her tongue against mine and it had a familiar feel to it. I don't have a conscious memory of feeling her lips against mine, but I knew that it had happened before. When my hands rolled down from her shoulders to the small of her back and onto her ass, I had a sense of Deja-vu. The smell and taste of the nape of her neck as I kissed her told me that there was something that I needed to remember, but I couldn't.

In that little pool next to the waterfall, Diane and I intertwined on both a physical and spiritual level. When I was inside of her it was like I was swimming through the stars. The spray from the water flowing from the rock showered us with a sense that everything in the world was right. For but a little blip in time, I had felt a little bit of acceptance that I had never felt before in this world. It was serene.

The next morning when I woke up in the tent, I had a strong feeling of anxiety. I couldn't quite put my finger on it. There seemed to be a little voice in the back of my head telling me that I needed to leave and get as far away from the gathering as possible. I unzipped the tent, stepped out and looked around. The sky seemed ominous, with dark low-level clouds that were almost fog. Campfires were still smoldering from the night before. The only other person that seemed to be awake at that early hour was some guy babbling incoherently just out beyond the line of trees. I couldn't really see him and I had no idea what he was talking about.

As I looked around, I had the sense that something just wasn't right. I crawled back into the tent and woke Diane up. "I think I need to leave this place," I told her.

"What's wrong?"

"I don't know. I just have a bad feeling. Something seems wrong."

"Where are you going?"

"Maybe I'll head for the coast. Do you want to come?"

She rubbed her eyes and stared back at me without answering my question. She crawled out of the tent naked and looked around. She walked over and sat on a log next to one of the smoldering fire pits. She seemed to be bathing in the smoke. She stared at me intently for a while then stood up and looked around at all of the other tents.

"I think I need to go see the ocean," I said.

She still didn't say anything. There was no emotion on her face. I wasn't going to wait for her decision. I cleaned out the tent and started tearing it down. I handed Diane her clothes and threw everything I had into the back of the jeep. She just kept sitting on the log staring at me as I went about my business. When everything was loaded up and I was about to put the key into the ignition I asked her again if she wanted to come with me.

She seemed suspicious of me. "I'll be back," she said. She walked to a tent that was about a hundred yards away and disappeared inside. In about fifteen minutes she walked back and threw a backpack into the back of the jeep and got into the passenger seat.

We didn't really have a plan about where we were going other than to the Pacific. I kept my eye on the floating-ball compass attached to the windshield. I tried to keep the jeep heading between "S" and "W" as much as possible. We decided to keep heading in that direction until we ran out of road.

Diane spoke in a strange manner. Most of the time we were driving, the two of us sat there in a comfortable silence. Other times it was like something possessed her and she couldn't quit talking. She wasn't one for small talk, if her mouth was open, she had something to say, usually it was something profound. She wasn't going to waste time talking about mundane shit about the weather or something she saw on television once. She might occasionally talk about a book, but other than that her words were of a mystical, almost other worldly matter. She was very much a free spirit, but in a troubled kind of way.

After three days of driving we reached our destination if that's what you wanted to call it. The pavement had come to an end and we were sitting in the jeep on top of a cliff overlooking the shimmering waves. We weren't really sure exactly where we were, we hadn't been paying a whole lot of attention to the highway signs. She thought that we were in southern Oregon, but I was fairly certain that were in northern California.

After a little looking around, we found a way to drive the jeep down on the beach. We found a place that was like a shallow cave. We decided that was where we were going to stay until we got restless and felt the need to move on. There was no place that we needed to be. Time meant nothing to us.

As I started to unload the jeep, she said "Stop. There will be plenty of time for that." She walked over to me and lifted my shirt off then took hers off too. I looked around and realized that there wasn't another living soul anywhere. It wouldn't have mattered if there was, it wouldn't have stopped her. She took my shorts and sandals off and I stood there naked.

She was soon naked too. Her blonde hair lingered down her tan body. She grabbed my hand and we started walking towards the surf breaking on the shore. There was nothing playful about what she was doing it was more calculated and methodical. We walked through the waves until we could no longer feel the sand beneath our feet.

"I love the feeling of floating," she said. "I love feeling the force of the tide push me around. You really get in touch with who you are out here."

The next two days were spent doing almost the exact same thing. At no point did we feel it necessary to even put clothes on. We stayed up late just talking around a fire, the days were spent walking along the beach or just lying in the sun. We fucked every few hours. I would never use the term "making love" to describe what we were doing. It was raw and primal. I think that in the short time that we knew each other, that we developed a feeling that others might define as love but that wasn't the way it really was. It was more like that the universe deemed it necessary for Diane and I to be together.

On our third night at the beach I woke up at what must have been an early morning hour but I couldn't be sure because neither of us had a watch or any other time measuring device. I wasn't sure what woke me up. It wasn't a dream, and I didn't recall hearing a sound, but my heart was pounding. Even though the mist of off the ocean made for a cool night I was soaked with sweat.

It was only a minute or two after my own awakening that Diane suddenly sat straight from the sleeping bag. Here face seemed to morph between panic and despair. "What the fuck did we do?" She screamed.

"I don't know. What do you mean?"

"We should never have left the gathering." There were tears rolling down her cheeks. "That isn't what was supposed to have happened."

"It seemed to me that it was kind of winding down anyway."

"They're all gone," she said, "but they didn't leave."

She got up and walked out of the tent, so I followed her. She stared up at the full moon for a long time, and then turned and looked at me. She started crying and walking around in circles.

Through her sobs, she kept muttering, "We should never have left. We should never have left. That was our destiny." The circles that she walked in kept getting bigger and bigger until she was walking onto the wet sand left by the receding waves. I followed her down to the water not so much as an attempt to console her but to try and understand what the fuck she was talking about.

As I got close to her she stopped crying and walking in circles and asked me if I would go back to the tent and get her a cigarette. Through the light of the moon I could see in her pupils some sense of peace. I gave her a half-hearted smile and said, "okay".

I walked back to the tent wondering what the hell was going on with this girl. I grabbed the cigarettes and a lighter and then turned to start walking back towards the water. By that time, she was waist deep in the surf. I stopped in my tracks and just watched her. Diane, on the other hand, didn't stop walking. I thought that she was going out there to float like she loved to do so much, but then through the darkness I could see that she started swimming. She was going in the opposite direction of me. In only a few moments, she escaped the lunar light and became invisible to me.

I lit one the cigarettes that was in my hand and then looked around the back of the jeep for a bottle of Mezcal that I knew was in there somewhere. Once I found it, I walked down to the water's edge and sat down. I sat there sipping and chain smoking the Marlboros. As the sun came up, I scanned the silvery horizon for any sign of Diane. As the day progressed, I walked up and down the coast looking for any trace of my week-long lover. She wasn't sunbathing on a rock, nor was there a body washed up on the beach. She was just gone.

That night I sat by the fire and watched the flames dance. If I heard a sound other than the roar of the waves crashing down below, I looked up to see if somehow Diane had found her way back to me. It was hope against hope. It wasn't like the two of us had ever had a plan once we left the beach, but now I had no plan whatsoever. I don't think that I had ever really felt connected to anybody else or anything else in the world, but it wasn't until that moment that I truly felt loneliness. In some ways I liked the feeling, there was a serenity to it. I could spend a couple more days on that beach until I figured out what I was going to do next.

That night as I slept in the tent, I had one of my "Terminal" dreams. As usual, it was the same place but had a different atmosphere from my previous excursions there. It was extremely busy, hundreds and hundreds of people going in all different directions, yet despite all of this there was very little noise. Most of the people there only seemed to have passing conversations.

I sat down on one of the long black benches that sparsely populated the place and just watched all of the people pass by me. Some of them made eye contact with me, but most seemed oblivious to my existence. There were a lot of people who looked gravely ill. Many of them looked very angry or mean. Occasionally I would see somebody with a smile on their face and looked really happy.

After a few moments of watching the masses head in all different directions around me, I saw a face that I recognized. I remembered him from the gathering. We had had a few beers together and a great conversation about just random shit. We had made plans to get together for more drinking, but because Diane and I had decided to make an abrupt departure for the west coast. I wasn't sure if I couldn't remember his name or was never introduced.

He must have recognized me too, because he walked straight towards me. He had a puzzled look on his face. "What are you doing here?"

"I don't know. I think I'm dreaming."

He stared at me blankly. I thought he was going to start laughing, but he never did. "There are no such things as dreams," he said. "You are simply at a different coordinate in the universe."

I kind of nodded to him and said, "if you say so".

"Look man, everything is equally real," he said. "Everything is equally unreal too."

"What are you doing here?" I asked him.

"Can't you tell by looking?"

I looked at him. He looked the same way he had at the gathering. He was even wearing the same thing, flip flops, tank tops and shorts made out of cut up army pants. "You look the way I remember you."

"You're not looking hard enough," he said. As he spoke, I noticed a huge wound in the side of his head. It looked like it had been bashed in by a rock.

"They don't want us here Vincent," he said as turned and started walking away.

"Who doesn't want us here?"

"That's something you are going to have to figure out on you own."

I watched him walk away until he faded out of sight.

++   ++   ++

When I woke up from the dream, the sun was just beginning to cast pink sparkles on the ocean through the light fog. As my morning grogginess was wearing off, I begin to feel a sense of panic. Just like that morning at the gathering I had a strong feeling that I needed to be somewhere else. I wasn't sure where, but I needed to get moving. My skin was tingling with restlessness. I walked down the beach, not at a leisurely pace, but with a determination to get to an unknown destination.

As I walked, I remembered the experience that I had during my sleep. I thought about the wound on the side of the guy's head, his parting words to me and trying to figure out exactly who he was talking about when he said, "they don't want us here." Why did he use the term "us"? I came to the conclusion that I needed to go back to where the gathering was being held. I needed to know what, if anything, had happened there.

I packed up the jeep and just started driving. As I drove, things started making sense to me. I was getting a little nervous because I was sure that something very bad had happened there. I thought that Diane must have had a vision about what was going on there and that was why she walked into the ocean and never came back. That was why the guy in the Terminal in my dream had his skull crushed.

I pushed that jeep as hard as it would go. I paid very little attention to the scenery around me. I had but a single vision as I drove and that was to find out what had happened at the gathering. I needed to know who it was that didn't want me here. I had worries that I wouldn't be able to find the site again.

My worries were completely unfounded. I went directly to the place, like the jeep was driving itself. As I drove down into the valley, I noticed that there wasn't a single soul around. There were tents still set up, and some of the fire pits still smoldered. It wasn't until I got closer that I noticed the place was in disarray. Tables were knocked over and all of the vehicles that were there had their windows smashed out. Still, there wasn't a single person around.

I parked and got out to walk around. I started to notice all of the blood stains. They were everywhere. There were big spots on the ground, there were several of them. Most of the tents had splatter stains on them. There were no bodies though. I saw what appeared to be small pieces of flesh here and there. It was obvious that people had died, but I had no guess as to what happened to the carcasses.

As I looked around, it occurred to me that nobody knew what happened here except whoever was responsible for it. I didn't see any evidence that the police or fire department had ever been there. I walked all around the grounds but couldn't make any sense of what had happened, only that some type of slaughter of the people at the gathering had taken place. The air had the faint smell of rotting meat.

A sense of fear came over me as I started hearing sounds from the trees on the mountain. I listened intently. It wasn't the wind, and it didn't seem to be an animal. As the sound grew closer it became evident that it was a person walking through the trees. You could hear the footsteps.

I looked around for something to use as a weapon. I had no idea whether the person was someone who had survived the massacre or somebody who had committed it. My options for protection were limited to sticks and rocks. I found a rock with a sharp point and started walking directly towards the noise. It wasn't much of a plan; I was just acting on instinct.

As I got to the edge of the trees, I could see a figure about fifty feet in front of me. It wasn't moving aggressively so I relaxed a little and waited. As he got closer, I realized that it was Miles.

"I've been expecting to you," he said.

"What happened?"

"I'll tell you later. We need to get out of here now."

Before we left, Miles and I scavenged the campsite for anything we might need. We took all of the food, alcohol, cigarettes and drugs that we could find. We found a few dollars here and there, but not a substantial amount.

"There is a ranch in Utah that I need you to drive me too," he said. "Take anything you might need."

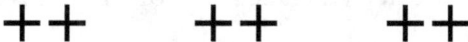

I didn't know what to make of Miles as we drove the winding dirt road up out of the valley. Part of me that was suspicious of him. I wasn't sure that I wanted to go to whatever ranch he wanted to go to. At that point I wasn't sure if he was a friend or an enemy. He wasn't saying anything. I looked over at him and he was just staring down at the place where the gathering had been. He shook his head and closed his eyes. He muttered something about needing to get to another place and another time before it was too late.

It was about an hour on our drive south that Miles seem to snap out of the state of consciousness he was in. I never thought that he was sleeping, but he never really seemed to be there either. He reached into the backpack at his feet and pulled a joint out. He lit it and took a long hit. He held the smoke in for a long time before he blew it out, then handed it to me. I mimicked what he had done, and then handed it back to him.

"Why did you leave the gathering?" He asked me.

"I met a girl while I was there. We did some mushrooms and went up to a waterfall. We had sex and then went back to my tent. In the morning when I woke up, I felt a sense of dread. I had a feeling that something bad was going to happen. I felt like I needed to get out of there. I asked her she wanted to go with me. We ended up driving out to the ocean."

"Where is she?"

"She's gone." He didn't say anything, so I continued, "she had a dream or a vision or something. She knew that something happened at the gathering. She kept saying that we should never have left the gathering. That it was our destiny to be there. She was distraught about whatever she thought had happened there, and to make a long story short, she ended up swimming out into the ocean and that was the last I saw of her."

"What about you?", he asked. "Did you have any dreams or visions?"

"I had dream, but it didn't seem like a dream, it was like I was somewhere else. In it, I had met a guy who I had a few beers with around a fire at the gathering. In the dream, he had a huge hole in the backside of his head. He said something about somebody not wanting people like us here."

Miles didn't say anything to me as I spoke, but I could tell by the look on his face that he was understanding everything I was saying to him. The look in his eyes assured me that he had been through something similar.

"What happened there?", I finally had the balls to ask him. He raised is eyebrows in such a way that I knew that it wasn't something that he was ready to talk about, and looked away from me for a while.

"The shadows came," he finally said.

"The shadows?"

"I had a feeling that they would be coming this time. I knew some old friends of mine would be staying in the trees. I've known them forever. Even at a gathering of like minds, there were a few of us that were even more like minded. One of the guys calls us the council."

He took a hit off of the joint and handed it to me. "A couple days after you left," he said, "me and the guys were sitting around the fire tripping acid. We started hearing screams. One of the guys started laughing and said 'the shadows have arrived'. We clicked out bottles of tequila together in a toast."

"I guess you guys were ready for it," I said.

"All of us have been through a purge before. I guess that's why we always searched each other out at gatherings. I know that purges are necessary, but I guess we really shouldn't have been celebrating it."

"Who are the shadows?"

"I thought the guy in your dream in explained that to you."

"No. He didn't explain anything. He just said that they didn't want us there. He never said who 'they' were."

Miles laughed. "It sounds to me like everything was precisely explained to you."

After that, the conversation was sparse between us as we drove. He would occasionally give me directions. I liked the fact that the old man wasn't one for small talk. He wasn't going to waste his words on shit that didn't matter.

As we neared our destination somewhere in Utah, he told me about the place we were going to. "When I got back from Vietnam, someone told me about a ranch in the middle of nowhere that needed some workers. After the war, I figured that the middle of nowhere was exactly where I wanted to be."

After several miles of driving a rutted dirt road, we came to a gate. Miles reached into his backpack and pulled out a small metal tin with a key inside of it. He got out of the jeep, unlocked the chains securing the gate and motioned me to drive through the gate. He locked the gate behind me and when he got back into the jeep, he handed me the tin and told me to keep it in a safe place.

The road we were driving on slowly turned into a canyon around us. I started noticing some structures of some kind. I realized that we were in some kind of ghost town. It almost seemed like there should be people there, but you could tell that nobody had been there in a long time.

Miles told me to stop the jeep. "This is it," he said. "The final destination."

I got out and looked around. The buildings on the canyons floor looked like houses that had been built around a dug-out pit. There were clay jars and bowls strewn about the ground. I looked up towards the top of the cliff and saw what appeared to be even more houses. I had the feeling that I was only one of a few people that had been there in a couple of hundred years.

Miles wasn't saying anything, and I had the feeling he didn't want to talk so I didn't press the issue. He started to gather up wood and threw it into a deep pit. He kept bringing pieces of wood to the pit until it was full. He pulled out a match and soon the flames were above our heads. Miles grabbed his backpack and threw it into the fire. He stripped off his clothes and threw them into the pit as well. He sat down naked on a rock and watched as every possession that he owned burned.

"Over a thousand years ago," he finally spoke, there was a society of people that flourished here, but then they just disappeared."

"From the looks of it, it happened pretty fast."

"Do you see those rooms up on the cliff?" he asked.

"Yes."

"There must have been something down here that scared the hell out of those people."

"Probably animals, or enemies."

"Or shadows." As the sun sat Miles starting walking up to the top of the cliff. I knew that he wasn't going to be coming back down. I grabbed a baggy of mushrooms from the jeep and ate a handful. "It's been a pleasure know you in this world," I shouted out to me friend. "See you in the next one."

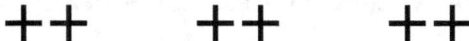

I looked over at the girl sleeping on my air mattress. I opened another beer, lit another cigarette, and it occurred to me how smug I was feeling about myself. I gazed amazingly at her naked body and thought about the amazing sex I had just had with this beautiful woman who was probably just a little north of being half of my age. I couldn't help but wonder why she had ever agreed to come home with me. If it had only been about getting laid, I was fairly certain that she could have done far better than me. Certainly, she could have found a guy around her age who would have had more stamina than a broken-down alcoholic, cocaine fiend.

I couldn't help but wonder what her motive was. I decided that I didn't give a fuck what her motive was. I just needed to enjoy the moment that I was in. I wanted to be next her. I wanted neither of us to feel lonely again. I crawled onto the mattress and put my arm around her.

I softly ran my hand over her body. She gave a soft hum of approval. As I caressed her lower back and slid my fingers across her ass, I had a sense that I had been with this girl before. It defied common sense, because I was certain that I had never seen her face before. Still, I felt an aura of familiarity.

As I pulled her close to me and kissed the back of her neck, there was scent I smelled that took me back to a place that I had been before. I couldn't put my finger on that place, but it wasn't a foreign place. It was just a place that was burned into my mind, I just couldn't figure out where it was.

I wanted to wake her up and ask her why I was feeling what I was feeling, but I knew all of those answers would come at some point. I decided that it would only ruin the peaceful feeling I was experiencing as we lay naked together supported only by a bed of air and slightly covered by a ratty afghan that was riddled with holes burned by errant cigarettes I had lit while I was half asleep.

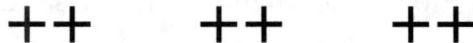

I guess that sometime during my mushroom trip I decided it was a good idea to sleep naked in a dry creek bed, at least that's how I woke up. Despite the heat in the desert, a chill ran through my body. Just like after the time drinking Ayahuasca, I woke up with a long beard. As I lie there, the morning sun was soon smothered out by fast moving thunderhead clouds. There was a big storm coming. The wind kicked up out of nowhere and the sand started hitting my naked body so hard that it burned. It was getting in my eyes and I could barely see. I threw everything into the jeep and started driving. I knew that I wasn't going to be able to outrun the storm and steered right into it.

Once I got through the weather, it occurred to me that I had no idea where I was going. I had no real home to return to, but I knew that I couldn't continue to just wander through life. I was getting low on money and needed to come up with some type of idea. It was harder for me than it might sound, because I had never given any real thought to my future. I wasn't even sure if I had one. The only thing I knew for sure at that point was that I wanted to be near the ocean. The jeep was already moving in the southwest direction. It seemed as good way to go as any.

After almost two days of driving, I ended up in a little section of San Diego called Ocean Beach. I bought a newspaper as soon as I got into town. As I looked through the classified ads it soon became clear to me that I wasn't going to be able to afford a real place to live. I had less than a couple of hundred dollars to my name, but as I looked out from the pier, I knew that this was the only place that I wanted to be. I had the feeling that it was somewhere that I needed to be for whatever reason.

I spent the next week living out of the jeep in parking lots around the beach. When the cops hassled me about being there too long, I just moved to a different lot. There was a large homeless population in the area. They were mostly young adults about my age. I started becoming friends with some of them. During the day, we would hang out under the pier and get high. At night we would sit around one of the fire pits on the beach and drink cheap wine. I was captivated hearing the stories of my new friends' lives. Most of them were sad and tragic, but I still liked them.

I became friends with a surfer who called himself Leno. He was a classically good-looking guy with long sun-bleached blonde hair and almost always had a smile on his face. He was always very generous with his weed and we smoked quite a bit of it my first few days there. As we smoked a bowl one day, he asked me where I lived.

"Over there." I pointed towards the jeep.

"I have a big house a few blocks away," he said. "There are a lot of other people that live there. It's almost like a commune."

"That sounds pretty cool."

"There's a closet that we could rent to you."

"A closet?" That made me laugh.

"I know." He laughed too. "It's a good-sized closet. The last girl that was in there had a twin bed in it."

"I don't have much, so I guess I don't need much. And I am sick and tired of sleeping in the jeep."

I sold the jeep, gave Leno a couple of month's rent and still had enough left over to keep me floating until I found a job working as the bar back and dishwasher at an Irish pub over on Newport Boulevard. The owner of the place was a good guy and I was allowed to help myself to as many drinks and cheeseburgers as I wanted.

I like Leno almost immediately. He was very introspective and spoke in soft, measured words. His constant smile was infectious. For somebody so young, it seemed to me that he had everything all figured out. It was like he was truly at peace with himself. I asked him how he always seemed so content with himself.

"It comes from watching the waves," he said. "There is just something about the movement of the ocean that is so perfect. It might look like violent chaos to most people, but everything about it is perfect harmony. The ocean is like one big synchronized dance of a trillion people, and when I look at it the whole world just seems to make sense. If you are in tune with the ocean, then you are in tune with everything, you can feel all space and time."

Leno's room was in the attic. As expected, it was filled with surfboards, but he also had so many books that filled the shelves and there were still piles on the floor. There was a mattress on the floor and a recliner in the corner. There were sliding glass doors leading out to a small wooden balcony that he had built himself.

One night we were sitting on that balcony drinking beers and smoking a joint when I asked him, "what do you mean when you say that you feel all space and time when you are watching the ocean?"

He studied my face for a while. I could tell that he was wondering if I would be able to understand what he was about to say to me. He stood up and pointed to the screen door. "Stare at this screen for a moment."

"Okay."

"Let's say this screen is the universe. I know this screen has a frame, but the universe doesn't. It is endless. There are an infinite number of strands that run vertical and an equal number of strands that run horizontal. The vertical strands represent the entirety of space, and the horizontal strands are the all of time. Every time that a horizontal strand meets a vertical one, it is an intersection in the universe."

He stopped himself, and shook his head. "I'm sorry," he said. "I hate when I say that."

"Say what?"

"Universe. That implies that there is only one universe. There are an infinite number of universes. They all interact with one another. What I mean to call it is the 'multiverse'. There are a billion different versions of us having almost this same conversation, the only difference is that each universe come with its own set of intricate variables."

Once again, he stopped speaking and stared at my face. "I follow what you're saying," I said.

He pointed back to the screen. "Okay, this screen is the multiverse. The top third is the future. The middle part is the present, and the bottom third is the past. Focus in on just one of these intersection of strands. Did you pick one?"

"Yeah."

"Show me which one it is."

I got up and pointed to an intersection almost in the exact center of the screen. "This one".

"That is where your soul is at right now. But with a little training, you can maneuver your soul into almost any other intersection on this screen. You don't have to be trapped in one universe."

"You said 'almost' any other universe. Why not all of them?"

"I'm not really sure. It's just a feeling that I have. I think there are certain universes where certain souls don't belong. They are like dead zones. Any given universe can kill a soul."

"Holy shit, I get it. I know exactly what you are saying. I've always had this feeling that that was the way it was, but I was never able to find the words to describe it".

Leno sat back down, lit the joint and passed it to me. We just sat there in a stoned silence for a while. A sense of liberation washed over me.

I looked out over the neighborhood below us. "Leno, if you built this deck yourself, why did you did you build it facing inland? I thought you would have built it on the west side so that you could see the ocean and watch the waves like you do so much."

He shook his head in disagreement. "That's a perceptive question. I just don't want to get spoiled and take the ocean for granted. The moments I have with the water are sacred to me. Whether I'm surfing, or sailing, or just watching the breakers crash onto the sand. Besides, he looked to the east, that is the direction I need to be wary of. That's where all the threats come from. That's where all the bad is."

"Why do you think that?"

"For some reason, in this intersection of the multiverse, there are too many beings that shouldn't be here. This is a dead zone for a lot of souls and they don't even realize it."

He told me that he wanted to go to bed. He wanted to be up early in the morning because the surf was supposed to be really good. I thanked him for everything and went to shake his hand. Instead, he pulled me close and kissed my neck. His hand slid beneath my shorts and felt my ass as said goodnight. It wasn't what I was expecting, but I was surprised that I felt no objection. I slowly ran my hand over his chiseled chest and walked out of the room.

I crawled into the sleeping bed on an old army cot in the closet. As I fell asleep, I thought about everything that Leno had said to me. I thought about the way he touched me. I wondered if I should have kissed him back.

++   ++   ++

My journey to the Terminal in my dreams was quite different that night. On my previous excursions to the place I had always had a somber feeling with a relatively low volume of noise. This time there was almost an aura of celebration. As I sat on one of the long black benches, I noticed that most of the people that passed by me had a smile on their face. There was a buzz in the air. If you listened hard enough, you might hear the occasional burst of laughter. Everybody walked faster and had a sense of direction in their step. It was like they all knew exactly where they were going.

Out of the corner of my eye, I could see some type of brightness. I turned to see what it was. There was a luminescent figure walking towards me. I felt a sense of excitement as it approached me, but I wasn't sure why. As the figure got closer, the brightness dissipated. I saw a smile that I recognized. It was Diane and she was walking right towards me. She looked beautiful. She moved with a sense of contentment and confidence that I had never noticed when we were together.

"Oh Vincent, I am so happy that you could be here," she said as she sat down on the bench and kissed me on the cheek. "I didn't think that you were going to make it. How have you been?"

I fumbled for words. "I'm still pissed at you."

"Awe," she said. "That's sweet".

"It's good to see you Diane. I've missed you."

"There is no need to miss me. I'm always here."

"Will you tell me why you walked into the ocean that night?"

She kind of rolled her eyes at me and said, "that was just how it was supposed to be. I was sure that you would understand. I was never meant to be on that beach in the first place."

"What do you mean?" I asked.

"I had always felt out of place in that life. I didn't want to feel that way anymore."

"You could have at least told me what you were going to do and say goodbye."

She stood up and said, "it's been good to see you Vincent".

"It's good to see you too Diane."

"I'm not going to say 'goodbye' this time either. Once you realize why I walked into the ocean you will know that there are no such things. We'll be seeing each other again."

And then she was gone, and I was awake.

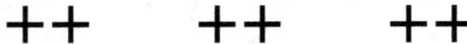

My life of sleeping in the closet wasn't as bad as it might sound. It was a big closet. The cot fit in there easily, and there was still plenty of room for every other material possession that I owned. The only time that I was ever really ever in there was when I passed out at night. The rest of the time was spent either at work, at the bar, or at the beach. I spent a lot of time fishing off of the pier.

When I was at home, it was a big enough house that we all had common areas to share. There was a living room, a good-sized kitchen, and a nice yard with the biggest table I had ever seen. We all took turns cooking for everybody else in the house and whoever else might have stopped by. As a resident of the house, it was required that you cook dinner on your designated night. The night that it was your turn to cook, you had to pay for everything, the food, the gallon jugs of wine, and you had to clean up and do the dishes when dinner was over. It could get expensive when it was your turn, but when it wasn't everything was free. You were basically a dinner guest.

There were eight of us in the house while I was living there, five guys and three girls. The guys, except for me, were all surfers. They did just enough work to pay for the basics in life. They didn't care a whole lot about anything else other than catching waves. Two of the girls that lived with us were also surfers and they were girlfriends of one of the guys that lived there.

The third girl that lived there was named Angela. She loved to party. She had dark curly hair and big tits that she loved to show off by wearing only an undersized bikini top most of the time. From what I could tell, she was pretty much a nymphomaniac. The girl loved sex. I think that every guy who lived in the house, including the two with girlfriends would walk into her room and stay for some time. I could hear the loud moans whenever Leno walked behind the door. It wasn't limited to the guys that lived in the house. There were always strangers walking in and out of her room. If she went out at night, she would usually bring home somebody I had never seen before, and probably wouldn't see again.

One time while I was asleep on the cot in the closet, something woke me up in the early morning hours. In the haze of sleep, I realized that my dick was agonizingly hard. It was almost painful. When I became fully aware of what was going on, I realized that Angela was in the closet with me. She was alternately sucking my cock and licking my balls. After Angela knew that I was awake, Angela crawled onto the cot and straddled me. She guided herself onto me and just started riding it in a slow, deliberate, deep way. I think that we came at the same time, and when she did, she just said "Thank you" and left.

It wasn't long before I was scheduled into the steady rotation of guys walking in and out of her bedroom door. It wasn't only guys that passed into the room. Angela would occasionally bring a girl home after a night of partying. On one such night, Leno and I were smoking a joint on the balcony and we could hear the sounds coming from Angela's room below. The girl that she had bought home was very vocal, and obviously enjoying herself very much.

"Damn," Leno said to me. "I wish that I could eat pussy that well."

It was only a few nights later, in the middle of the night, that Angela opened the door to the closet. She rubbed her hand over my stomach and chest, and put her index finger over her lips to let me know not to say anything. "Be quiet," she said and grabbed my hand and led me up to her room.

I was already naked, because that was the way that I always slept. She was wearing a see-through gown that stopped right around the middle of her thighs. Once the door to her room was shut, she pulled the gown over her head and let it fall to the floor. I walked over to her but she put her palm on her chest to stop me. "Not yet," she said.

I shrugged my shoulders and said, "okay".

She just sat at on the side of the bed looking at me. I couldn't resist myself any longer and started walking towards her again. "Not yet," she said again.

"What's going on?" I asked.

"You'll see."

At almost the same time, Leno walked through Angela's door wearing only a skimpy pair of bikini underwear. Angela went over and sat in a chair in the corner. Without a word, he walked over to me and kissed me on the neck the same way he had that night we got high on the balcony. This time, however, his actions were a little bit more aggressive. I could tell by the look in his eyes that there was something about him that night.

I couldn't help but admire the aesthetics of Leno's lean, muscular, tanned body. I had never been attracted to a guy before, but he looked like a Greek god. He grabbed me by the hand and pulled me onto Angela's bed. The peaceful, introspective guy that I had always known Leno to be wasn't there that night. He told me to lay on my back, close my eyes, and relax. He started kissing my body all over until his mouth was giving me head. To this day, I'm not sure why, it just felt right. It was exhilarating. I briefly opened my eyes to look over at Angela sitting in the corner. She was fingering herself.

It felt great to have Leno's body intertwined with mine. I told him that it was his turn to lay on his back, close his eyes and relax. His body was like a work of art. I just looked him over and thought about how he had the perfect nipples for a man. I couldn't help but pinch them, and suck on them occasionally. We just started exploring each other's body. It was clear that neither of us wanted to penetrate each other in any way, but the attraction we held for each other was undeniable.

At some point Angela became either jealous, or turned on, because she crawled onto the bed and forced her way between us. I don't think that Leno or I minded in the least. We stopped focusing on each other and turned all of our attention her. We took turns pleasing her while the other guy watched.

These kinds of threesomes continued between Leno, Angela and I for months. Somewhere along the line, we started inviting the other guys that lived in the house to join us, even the guys that had girlfriends, and it simply became us gangbanging Angela. It wasn't long before the other girls in the house found out what was happening. To everybody's surprise, they were both pretty cool about what was going on. They wanted in on the action. After that, every night at the house became a full-on orgy. Everybody that lived there stripped naked as soon as they walked in the door. Even when we had dinner at the big table in the yard, we were all naked. We knew that the neighbors could see us, but we didn't care, and they didn't care either.

The sexuality that was going on at that house was epic. Everybody was fucking everybody. The guys were fucking each other. The girls were fucking each other. Every combination of people that lived in that house were fucking each other. Outsiders might have thought of it as a debaucherous situation, but they wouldn't have understood, so there was no reason to explain it to them.

Then there was the morning that everybody in the house woke up to the sound of loud screaming coming from Angela's room. She had received a call from somebody. Her dad had died. Everybody in the house asked her how it happened, but she didn't know. She said that she needed to go back to Colorado, and she wasn't sure when, or if, she would be back. She asked me if I would go back with her.

I wasn't sure if I wanted to go with Angela to her father's funeral. I would have felt a little guilty if I let her go through the grief all alone, but the truth is that I really felt no emotional connection to Angela at all. I liked her as a person, and most of the time she was cool to hang out with. More than anything, I loved fucking Angela. She was so uninhibited. She wasn't worried about morals or what people thought of her. She loved sex and wasn't afraid to say so.

We ended up getting into her old Datsun 240Z and headed out. The first day we stopped in Las Vegas. We could have made it further, but Angela said she needed to have a few drinks. That sounded good to me. We found a cheap little motel and casino right off the strip. After we checked in, we headed straight for the bar.

She took a sip off of her vodka and cranberry juice and said, "I'm really dreading seeing my family. I was really close with my dad, but if it had been anybody else in the family that had died there is no fucking way that I would be making this trip."

"I guess there must be some bad feelings there," I said.

"My mom is a psychotic fucking cunt. Just a drunken drug addict."

"Well, I guess I'm not looking forward to meeting her then."

"She was always beating on somebody in the house. If it wasn't me or my dad, it was my little sister or one of my four brothers."

"You're not looking forward to seeing any of them?"

"I guess it would be cool to see my little sister. We have not talked in a long time. We were never real close because of the difference in age. I'm curious to see how she turned out."

"What about your brothers?"

She stared at me coldly. I must have hit a nerve. "I guess I won't mind seeing my little brother. He never did anything to me."

"I'm sorry."

"For what?"

"It seems like I said something that I shouldn't have."

"My older brothers are pieces of shit." Angela's voice was monotone as she talked. "I was eight years old when my oldest brother started sneaking into my room in the middle of the night. At first he would only touch me and make me kiss his dick...."

"You don't have to tell me this."

She ignored me. "After a couple of months, he started penetrating me. Once my second oldest brother found out what was going on, he started coming to my room too. And then the third brother too. There were nights when all three of them came to my room at some point."

"Didn't you say anything to your parents?"

"My dad always worked the graveyard shift so he was never around when it happened. I never said anything to him because I was afraid that he would think that it was my fault and not love me anymore. I always suspected that my mom knew, but she was just too drunk or high to give a damn."

"Oh God, Angela"

"When I was 16, I left that house and never went back. It was the morning after all three of my brothers came into my room at the same time. They kept laughing as they took turns raping me. They tied me up and used a miniature baseball bat on my pussy and ass."

"Nobody knows?"

"They do. And now you do too. It took me a few days to hitchhike to California and I haven't been back to Colorado since."

The next day we drove from Las Vegas to the house that she grew up in in Grand Junction. When we pulled up in front of the house, I could see Angela's hand start to shake.

"I don't want to do this yet," she said.

"Let's go find a motel room. We can deal with it in the morning."

After we unloaded our stuff into the room, Angela said that she was going to go out for a while. In about an hour she came back with some hamburgers, a newspaper and a half gallon of really cheap vodka. She handed me the greasy bag of food and started flipping through the paper. Pretty soon she crumbled up the paper and threw it into the corner. She started crying. "Godammit, there's no fucking obituary."

"Maybe it will be in tomorrow's paper."

"Maybe. I was hoping I could just find out where the funeral was going to be so I wouldn't have to go over to the house."

Angela unscrewed the cap off the vodka and started chugging it. Before my eyes I realized that I was seeing a side of Angela that I had never seen before. It was a side that I suspected never even existed.

On all of the occasions that I had had sex with Angela, she had always been fairly passive, almost submissive. It was like she was just along for the ride, and I, or Leno, or whoever else, could do anything they wanted to her. But that night in that motel room in Grand Junction, in an extremely intoxicated state, Angela became the aggressor. It was like she was possessed. She ripped my shirt off and pushed me down on the bed. After she got naked, she pulled my shorts off and climbed on top of me. She rode me so hard I was worried that she was going to break my dick. She was scratching me deeply with her sharp nails and bit my nipple so hard that there was a little blood.

I tried to push her off of me, but she wasn't having it. She kept thrusting herself down on me in a violent fashion. I finally felt her body start to shudder and I knew that she was on the verge of orgasm. I ended up cumming inside of her at the same time. She rolled off of me and we were both trying to catch our breath.

"I think you just got me pregnant," she said.

++ ++ ++

The next morning, I woke to the sound of Angela vomiting her guts out. She walked out the bathroom with puke still on the corners of her mouth, unscrewed the top off of the vodka and took a long swig. She stared at me with bloodshot eyes. I think that she was expecting me to say something, but no words came out. She walked back into the bathroom, shut the door, and I heard the shower turn on.

When she was done, she came out and said, "you need to take a shower before we go see my mom".

"I was planning on it."

"Take your time. I'm in no hurry. In fact, I'm dreading it."

When I got out of the shower, the bottle of vodka was empty sitting on the television. Angela was sitting in a chair staring out the window. She didn't acknowledge my presence.

We made the short drive over to the house. I was expecting to find a somber atmosphere, but it was anything but that. The place looked like there had been a party going on for days. The counter in the kitchen was full of empty beer cans and many had been used as ashtrays since the real ashtrays were overflowing with butts. The place was filthy, and it smelled that way too.

Her mother didn't even bother to get off of the couch when Angela and I walked in.

"I'm surprised to see you," her mother said. "The last I heard; you were living somewhere in California. I didn't think you would come all this way."

"I didn't come here to see you. I wanted to see dad one last time."

Her mom laughed. "Go make yourself a drink. You look like you could use one."

There were two of Angela's older brothers there. It was pretty obvious that they hadn't slept in a day or two. Their bodies were swaying even when they thought they were standing still. I could tell by the look in their eyes that they hated me from the second they saw me. They gave me the look of a scorned husband who had seen his ex-wife with a new boyfriend. I braced myself for some type of confrontation, but it never came.

As Angela and her mom talked about the funeral arrangements, the two brothers and I remained silent. It occurred to me that the conversation they were having was like a business meeting. There was no sharing of memories about the deceased. The tone of their voices was matter of fact. The funeral was going to be the next day. Then the day after the funeral, Angela was supposed to go meet with an attorney. She had no idea that her father had named her the executor of his will. I think that Angela was surprised that her father even had a will.

It was a relatively small funeral. Angela's mother and brothers sat on one side of the chapel in the mortuary with scattered people sitting behind them. Angela's little sister wasn't there. Nobody knew where she was or how to get in touch with her. Angela and I both noticed that sitting across the aisle was woman who was maybe forty sitting with two girls who looked like they were about to become teenagers. They kept their eyes looking straight ahead, just staring at the casket in front of them. There was an older couple sitting behind them. They too kept their eyes looking forward, never acknowledging anybody else in the room. I couldn't help but notice that Angela's mother kept giving dirty looks to the five strangers on the other side of the aisle. I could tell there was a lot of animosity between the two sides. I whispered to Angela asking who they were, but she didn't know.

After the funeral was over, everybody just went their separate ways. There were no handshakes, there were no hugs, and there was barely even a goodbye to be heard. Angela and I went back to the motel room. She immediately collapsed on the bed, and was asleep as soon as her head hit the pillow. She had pretty much been drinking nonstop since we got into town, and she had just buried her father. I poured myself a drink, lit a joint and turned on the television. I figured that Angela needed a rest.

The next morning, I was up early and Angela was still asleep. I took a shower, got dressed, and figured that I would just go walk around the town. I had never been to Grand Junction before, but from what I could tell it looked like a pretty cool place. When I was about to walk out the door Angela asked me where I was going. When I told her, she said not to be gone too long because she wanted me to go to the lawyer's office with her. It wasn't something that I wanted to do, but I nodded in agreement.

When I got back from my walk, Angela was showered and ready to go. I stared at her for a while. She looked like the same person I had known since I met her, but there was something different about her eyes. It was like she was the same shell of a human that I had always known, but now it was inhabited by a different soul.

As we were driving to the lawyer's office she said, "I was right".

"About what?"

"I'm pregnant."

"Did you take a test?"

"I don't need to. I can feel it."

I just left it that. I didn't know what to say.

When we got to the attorney's office, I noticed that the lettering on the door said "Geoffrey Jacobs. Collections Attorney". We walked in and there was a half dozen people all on the phone talking in hostile voices. The lady at the front desk told us to have a seat and that Mr. Jacobs would be with us shortly. Angela and I just raised our eyebrows to each other, the whole atmosphere seemed very odd to us.

After a few moments, Mr. Jacobs came out to greet us. He asked us to follow him into his office and as we walked, he offered his condolences, "I apologize for not being able to make it to the funeral. I had a court appearance that couldn't get rescheduled".

"Thank you," Angela said. "Can I ask why we are in a collection agency?"

"I don't normally do wills. This was a favor to your father. We had known each other from the bar for years."

"Why did my father make me the executor of the will?"

"That was my idea," Mr. Jacobs said. "Let's face facts, everybody else in your family is a piece of shit."

Angela smiled. "Show me what documents to sign. We want to get back to San Diego. I'm pregnant and I want to get back home."

Mr. Jacobs kind of shook his head. He looked at Angela, then over to me, then back to Angela. "It's not that simple. At the funeral, did you happen to notice a woman with two little girls?"

"Yes." Angela said.

"That was your dad's other family. This will is more than likely to have some complications. It would probably be cheaper for you in the long run to stay in town for a little while. There are going to be issues that we will need to discuss over the next few weeks."

As we got up to leave, Mr. Jacobs asked me, "Are you the proud father?"

"I guess." It wasn't the way that I wanted to answer the question, but it was the best thing I could come up with.

"Supporting a family can get expensive. What kind of work do you do?" he asked me.

"A little bit of everything." I said.

"What are you going to do while you're in Grand Junction?"

"I hadn't really thought about it. I assumed we would be on our way back to Ocean Beach by now."

"Why don't you come to work for me? We can train you to it, and if you're good at it, you can make a lot of money."

"I guess I have nothing to lose."

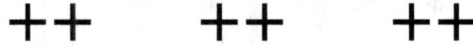

It turns out that I was a natural born bill collector. I was good at it. For the first time in my life, it seemed like the universe had a plan for me. I was destined to be on the phone all day hounding people for money, at least until the baby was born.

The owner of the agency, Geoffrey Jacobs, was a big, burly Jewish guy. It was like he was incapable of speaking in a normal tone of voice, he was always yelling. He would get pissed off over nothing and just start firing people at whim. Usually when he was the most pissed off is when he had lost a huge bet the night before. The guy loved to gamble.

I don't think that Angela had any clue what she was supposed to do as a pregnant woman. She went about her life as she always had. It was obvious that she was pissed off about being pregnant in the first place. She even told me that she was dreading having a baby, but the thought of having an abortion was even worse.

She was drunk one night and started punching me in chest, "what have you done to me?" she said through angry tears. "What the fuck have you done to me?"

"I don't like this either Angela"

It seemed like she needed to her me say the words, because it calmed her down. "Everything is going to work itself out," she said. "Everything will go exactly as it was meant to be."

The job at the collection agency was the first real job that I had ever had. I had never thought that I would have the type of job that I would go into an office and work. I had always figured that I would do something outdoors, and outside of the world of how normal people made money. All of that flies out the window when you think about having a child on the way.

The work wasn't hard at all. I would walk in in the morning, sit down at my desk and start calling people demanding that they send me money. I would call people about their phone bills, or their utility bills, or unpaid credit card. There was nothing that the collection agency wouldn't call you about. If a client wanted us to collect money for them, we would happily do so in return for keeping one third of the money that came in the door.

Like I said, the work itself wasn't difficult, but the environment was similar to working in a sweat shop. Each collector was under constant pressure to get money in the door. Mr. Jacobs could be a real dick. At the time, there were very few rules about how you could collect money. Threatening debtors with everything from lawsuits to jail was common place. We would lie, cheat and sometimes steal if that's what it took to get money through the door.

The reason for all of the evil was because if you weren't putting money into the agency's bank account you weren't going to have a job for very long. The money was counted at the end of each day, and you better have met your goal. If one day you missed your goal, you would pretty much just get a dirty look. If two days in a row you didn't hit your goal, you would get pulled into Mr. Jacobs' office and get screamed at for half an hour. If for three days in a row you failed at the goal, you would be given a paycheck and be told not to come in the next morning.

I guess I was lucky enough to have never had three bad days in a row. I was called into Mr. Jacobs' office and screamed at a few times, but on the third the money would come rolling in and I would start the whole process over again. The pursuit of the dollar was never ending. In a way, it's like a drug. It's all I thought about. I thought about money on my way to work, and I was thinking about it when I closed my eyes to go to sleep at night.

If life at work wasn't stressful enough, life with Angela was even worse. I'm not sure it was because she was pregnant, or that her dad had died recently, or if it was because she was living too close to a toxic family, but she wasn't the same person that I had traveled with from San Diego. Somewhere between then and now, a fundamental change had swept over Angela. She was so detached from not only me, but from the rest of the world as well. There were more than a few days that I would come home work and she would look at me as if she didn't know me.

We never talked about the fact that we were about to become parents. I was almost ambivalent about being a father. It was just something that was happening to me. I was being forced into it by my own actions. I was going to have to pay for it, cause and effect. I think part of the reason for my lack of enthusiasm was because I had never pictured myself as the type who was supposed to bring another person into this world.

I have never met anyone as miserable as Angela was while she was pregnant. It was easy to dismiss as simply the physical distress of carrying a child, but as the months rolled by, I realized that it was something deeper. She was chain smoking cigarettes and I rarely saw her without a tumbler of vodka in her hand. Her eyes changed color from the time she got pregnant. When I first met Angela, her eyes were silvery blue and radiated light. Somewhere along the line they became dark and shadowy. We rarely spoke to each other. We were living separate lives. On most nights, I slept on the couch.

That is where I was one night when something woke me up. I lay there for a moment listening. There was a sound coming from the bathroom. I heard something thumping. There was grunting and heavy breathing. As I got up to see what was going on, I could hear Angela sobbing. I knocked on the door, but she didn't answer. I asked her if everything was alright, but she still didn't say anything.

I slowly opened the door and the first thing that I noticed was all of the blood on the floor. Angela was sitting naked on the floor against the sink, and she was in some kind of catatonic state. Her eyes were rolled back in her head, and there was some kind of liquid running out the corner of her mouth. Between her legs was a blood mass that I soon realized was our child. I checked both Angela and the fetus, neither seemed to be moving.

After the ambulance left, I grabbed some things that I thought Angela might need and headed for the hospital. I was in a daze. I felt like I wasn't even in my own body. I barely remember the drive to the emergency room. When I got there, it was as if I just floated through the door. I knew there were a couple of people talking to me, but I couldn't hear what they were saying.

"Were you the husband?"

Nothing.

"Were you Angela's husband?"

Still nothing.

"Sir, we need to know if you were the husband and the father."

Slowly I became aware that at nurse was talking to me. I looked at her. "Yes," I said.

She had tears in her eyes. There was a doctor standing next to her. He shook his head and said, "I'm sorry".

"They're dead?"

"Your wife just lost too much blood. The child never had a chance. They're both gone. Would you like to spend some time with them?"

"No." I turned and walked out of the hospital.

As I drove home, I couldn't decide how I was supposed to feel. There wasn't any natural emotion coming to me. It would be easy to say that I was numb, but that wasn't the case. I literally had to make a decision about what emotion to have. I thought about Angela. It was hard to mourn her at that point. After all that we had been through, I didn't think I even knew her anymore. She was a stranger.

I thought about the fetus. The only thought that came to mind was, "lucky bastard".

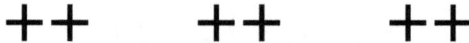

The night of Angela's funeral, I crawled into bed completely exhausted from the previous few days. It seemed like only a mere few seconds after my head hit the pillow that I found myself in one of my Terminal dreams. The place was nearly empty. The few people that were there were all very far away from me. They were all walking very slowly, and none of them seemed to walk with any sense of purpose. They all seemed lost.

I saw one figure that was probably a hundred yards away from me that was just standing still. Even from the distance, I felt a sense of familiarity about the figure. I started walking towards it. As I got closer to it, I realized that it was a guy about my age. I knew him from somewhere. He didn't seem aware that I was even approaching him. It was the kid who had lived at the house with me and the old woman when I was young, Xavier.

"Hello," I said to him.

He looked at hard at me hard for a moment. "Vincent?"

"Yes."

"It's been a long time."

"Yes, it has. What are you doing here?"

"I don't have clue," he said looking about the place. "I don't even know where I'm at".

"I've been here a few times," I told him.

"Where are we?"

"I haven't really figured that out. It seems to be some type of station. People seem to come here as they pass from one place to another."

This seemed to puzzle him at first, then his eyes got really big as if he had just had some type of epiphany. "This is everybody," he said. "This is the whole world."

"Why do you say that Xavier."

"Every soul in all existences is here right now."

I looked around the sparsely populated room, then back at him.

"Souls are like cars," he continued. "There are only so many makes and models. There are countless variations, and cosmetic changes are constantly being made, but when all is said and done, each soul has its own core."

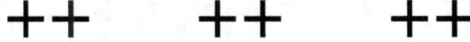

I woke up from the dream about Xavier feeling confused. I was confused by what he said. What the fuck was he talking about? I was also confused about what I was going to do with my life at the moment. With Angela dead, there was no reason for me to stay in Grand Junction any longer. Mr. Jacobs at the collection agency told me that I could take as much time off as I needed after her death, but I knew that it was all bullshit because without me on the phone there wouldn't be any money coming through the door. I didn't care. I no longer had to worry about caring for a family. I was fairly certain in my decision that I wouldn't be going back to that place.

There was a map of the United States in the glove compartment of Angela's Datsun 240Z. I pulled it out and just stared at it for a little while. My first thought was to drive back to San Diego, but I quickly realized that I didn't want to talk to Leno or anybody else about what had happened. I looked at the big dot that represented Las Vegas. Angela and I had stayed there on our way to Colorado, but it didn't feel like the type of place that I would fit into. Salt Lake City was out of the question. The weather in Tucson might be nice, but it seemed like it would be boring for some reason. I had never been to Albuquerque, and that alone made it somewhat appealing.

I had been to Denver once when I was a kid, and from what I could remember it seemed like a pretty cool place. I had never intended on driving east, but the Mile-High City was only three and a half hours away. I could be there before the sun was set. That was it. I loaded up the car and headed towards the mountains on Interstate 70.

When I got to Denver, I checked into a dingy little hotel room for the night. I chose the place because it was right next to a bar. I walked over and had a few beers while I thought about what it was, I was actually going to do in Denver. I had a little bit of money, but by the time I paid for a place to live, there wasn't going to be much left. I would have to worry about that in the morning, because, for that night, I was determined to get shit faced drunk.

With my head still throbbing in the morning, I stumbled a block or two to a convenience store for a newspaper and a cup of coffee. Back in the motel room, I opened the paper to the "housing" section. There was a studio apartment for rent in the southwest part of town that was in my price range. I went and looked at it and immediately gave the landlord the first and last month's rent as well as a couple hundred more for a damage deposit. It wasn't much, but it was fairly clean and after all I had been sleeping in a closet in San Diego.

After unloading what very little I had in the car, I opened the newspaper again, but this time I went to the "help wanted" section. I purposely didn't look for jobs in the collections field, because that wasn't something I ever wanted to do again. After looking through all of the other ads it occurred to me that working at a collection agency was the only thing that I was qualified to do, unless I wanted to return to being a bar back like I had been in San Diego. There was one ad that said, "interview today, start tomorrow". Despite the feeling in my gut telling me not to do it, it was something that I needed to do. I had enough money for the next month's rent, but that was about it.

In the morning I took a shower, put on my best shirt and tie and decided to bite the bullet and go fill out an application. The decision put me in a depressed state as I walked down to the car. I didn't want to do this. As I pulled out of the parking lot, I noticed that my new apartment was right across the street from a gentleman's club. I looked up at the marquee that read, "Under new ownership. Now hiring. All positions. Dancers. Bartenders. Doormen. Clean up crew".

I was already dressed up so there was no reason I shouldn't go in and at least talk to them. When I walked in it was still early. There was no music, and there were no girls dancing on the stages. There was just some guy sitting at a table counting money. I startled him when I walked in. He stood up and asked me what I wanted. I noticed that there was a gun in his belt that was fighting against the fat that was pushing it forward.

"I saw you sign outside," I said. "I need a job".

"You're not a dancer," he said. "Can you tend a bar?"

"I can pour a beer and mix a few drinks, but I'm a quick learner."

The fat guy shook his head. "I can tell by looking at you that you're not a janitor, so cleanup crew wouldn't work."

"Maybe not. At this point, I just need a job."

"How tough are you?"

"I'm not sure. I've never really been tested."

The fat guy laughed. "I guess you're big enough to be a doorman. When can you start?"

"Tonight."

"You're hired. Come back at six."

I could tell right away that working at the strip club was going to be an interesting experience.

The owner, Joe Q., as he liked to be called, was what most people would consider to be a sleazy street hustler, but he seemed pretty cool, and liked to have a good time. The girls that danced there were gorgeous, and more than a few of them were flat out crazy. The bartenders never charged us for our drinks. There was another doorman who worked beside me, then there were two other guys that did security inside the club. The clientele was diverse, guys from all walks of life who just liked to watch girls dance topless.

On my second night there, a guy handed me his ID. I looked at his age, then I looked at his name. It was Xavier whom I had just dreamt about a few nights earlier.

I looked him in the eyes. "Do you remember me?"

He looked at me for a few moments. "Is your name Victor?"

"Yes."

He smiled and shook my hand. "Man, it's been a long time. We need to catch up."

"I agree. Let's have drinks sometime."

"We'll figure it out." He started to walk into the club, then turned around suddenly. "It's funny," he said. "I just had a dream about you the other night."

After Xavier walked into the club, the doorman nudged me, "you need to be careful with that guy, he can get really crazy".

"Oh yeah," I said.

"We've had to escort him out of the place on more than a few occasions. The old owner tried to kick him permanently once, but the dancers complained that they couldn't get any cocaine."

"I think it will be okay. Xavier and I go way back."

Xavier started coming to my house after the club closed a few nights a week. He was small and skinny, with bulging eyes. I think that he was part Mexican. He liked to say that he was a musician. He would usually bring two or three of the dancers over and we would drink, snort lines and party until the sun came up. He never wanted to talk about our childhood, or basically anything about his past at all. The only thing he really cared about was partying. He seemed absolutely consumed by sex. If he wasn't fucking a girl, he was plotting how to get the next one to get in his bed. I was beginning to do as much cocaine as he did.

It became normal for there to be a party at my place almost every night after the club closed. Xavier always had a big bag of coke, which attracted the strippers like fish to a lure. He wasn't running a charity so he would invite other guys who were willing to pay for the cocaine so that Xavier could make a little profit, which at the time was basically his only source of income. I always had beer in the refrigerator and various bottles of liquor on the counter.

Xavier used to have one of the girls lay down naked on her stomach and proceed to cut lines on her ass. Once we all did all of the coke off of one girl, he would have another girl lay down and do the whole thing all over again. The girls were always up for whatever we wanted. It was almost a sure thing that I would get a blowjob every night. Sometimes I would fuck one of the girls while everybody was in a wired-up cocaine haze. Sometimes it would be an orgy and everybody was naked. Almost all of the dancers were bisexual and a couple of them would put on a lesbian show for us. Sometimes Xavier would bring just one girl over and we would take turns fucking her.

One night, while I was guarding the door, one of the security guys from inside the club grabbed my arm, "you need to come get Xavier. He's having a meltdown."

When I got to him, Xavier was extremely drunk. "Get the fuck off the stage," he screamed at one of the dancers. I looked at the girl, she must have been new because I had never seen her before. She was smiling at us, almost antagonizing Xavier.

"What's going on man?" I grabbed him by the jacket, "come on, I'll take you back to my place so you can sleep for a while".

"No, Victor." He broke away from me. "Don't you know who the fuck that girl is?"

I looked at the girl again. "No. I've never seen her before."

"It's the old lady. That's Anima."

Xavier's words startled me. That was the first time I had ever heard him call the woman from our childhood by name. "Nah man," I said. "She is probably long dead by now. Besides, look at that girl, she is young and beautiful."

"Goddammit Victor," he screamed. "Look at her. Really look at her. That's fucking Anima."

I looked at the girl again. She stared me down. There was a glint in her eyes, a familiar glint. Even though I had never seen the girl before, I knew her from somewhere.

At that point Joe Q. walked over to me, "Victor take the rest of the night off. I'll pay you, but I need Xavier out of this bar right fucking now." Joe Q. was pissed, and that wasn't his style. He was always laid back. He was a big, fat, always sweaty guy who always had that snub nose revolver in his waist band. He treated the club more like his personal playground than a business. He was constantly doing shots of tequila, and paying dancers to go into his office to give him head.

We went back to my apartment and Xavier walked straight to the bed and collapsed on it. There were tears streaming down his face.

"Are you alright?" I asked.

"No, I'm not alright. I've never been alright. I don't even know what 'alright' means."

"I guess I don't either."

"Do you remember the day that we all left the house?"

"Of course I do."

"Anima walked me out to a car that was waiting in the driveway. She told me that I need to get in the car. There was a lady in the driver's seat. Anima said she was going away and wasn't coming back. The lady in the car would take care of me. She drove me to this little cabin up in the mountains. As soon as we walked in the door, she told me to get undressed. She took me over to the bed and tied me down. She got naked too and got on top of me."

"Damn Xavier...."

"For the next few years, I became her sex slave. I guess there was a part of me that liked it. She was probably three times my age. We had sex every single night. She said that Anima had sold me to her."

"I don't know what to say."

"There is nothing that you can say."

Two nights later, Xavier was leaving the bar at three in the afternoon. He had been drinking there since they opened at seven in the morning. He was still wired from the night before. On his way to the next bar he ran a red light and broadsided a minivan. A father and two of his children were killed on impact. The mother and another child were critically injured. Xavier wasn't hurt at all.

The last time that I saw Xavier was through the glass at the jail as we talked over a phone. "My public defender says that I'm going away for a long time."

"That doesn't surprise me."

"You know what Victor; it doesn't really bother me that much. I don't think I ever really belonged in the outside world anyway. I don't know if I belong in any world."

"I'll come visit you again when I get the chance."

"Victor, don't take this the wrong way, but I don't want you to come see me again. I don't like the memories you make me have."

I took over selling coke to a few of Xavier's trusted customers. I didn't want to deal on the scale that he did, just enough to pay for what I was snorting and make a few extra dollars. One of the guys that came to buy from me was named Dave. He always showed up at the club around nine in the evening wearing a suit and tie. He was a nice enough, he just had a penchant for cocaine and big tits.

One night, when he came to get an eight ball from me, I asked him, "Why do you always have a suit on? What do you do for a living?"

"I'm the vice president of a bank. It sucks, but the pay is good. I couldn't get through the day without coke though. Too much stress."

"Why is that?"

"The board of directors put me in charge of starting up a credit card collections department. It's a pain in the ass."

"I know. I used to work at a collection agency."

His eyes lit up. "You need to come work for me."

"I don't know."

"I guarantee that I will make it worth your while."

"I hated doing collections. The only reason I did it was because I thought I was going to be a father."

He kept pleading with me and offering salary numbers. I kept saying no. He wouldn't take that for an answer, and the salary numbers got higher and higher. He finally got to that number that was too high for me to turn down. I told him that I would start in two weeks.

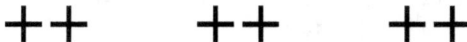

I was almost asleep when the girl next to me on my air mattress started talking. I was kind of annoyed because the cocaine that I had been snorting all night was starting to wear off and I felt like I was at the point where I thought I could get some sleep. I thought that she was actually saying something to me before I realized she was merely talking in her sleep.

As much as I wanted her to shut the fuck up and try to get some sleep, I couldn't help but listen to her. She kept saying, "the shadow is here, the shadow is here".

I wished that I could have just dismissed what she was saying, but I already knew who the shadows were. I just smiled as she repeated the phrase over and over. I got out of bed, sat back in the chair, and started chopping up what was left of the cocaine. I snorted a line, drank a beer, and smoked two cigarettes.

It occurred to me that I no longer cared whether I went to sleep that night. It simply didn't matter at that point.

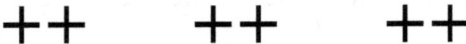

I had never pictured myself as the suit and tie kind of guy, but there I was. I took the bus into downtown Denver. I was just another face on the sidewalk dressed like a monkey until I got to the bank. I took the elevator up to the thirteenth floor and scurried into my cubicle and started making phone calls. There were hundreds of people on the floor doing the exact same thing. We were all calling people who had not paid their credit card bills.

The majority of people on the floor were calling people who had not paid their bill in a month. There was a slightly smaller group who had not paid their bills in two months. There were about forty people calling on accounts that had not been paid on in three to six months. I was part of a group of people who were calling people that had not made a payment in over 180 days. At that stage, they were no longer called customers, they were referred to as debtors and it was no longer about collecting payments. They owed the entire balance of the credit card.

For whatever reason, this line of work came naturally to me. I never took any of the business personally. It wasn't my money that the debtors weren't repaying. Unlike many of the other collectors on the floor, I could give a fuck whether the person on the other end of the line screamed at me or cussed me out. I never cared about the reason that people weren't paying their bills. I just wanted their money by whatever means necessary. It didn't matter if they were sick, or they were out of work, or there had been a death in the family, they just needed to put a check in the mail.

I was good at what I did, and I made a lot of money doing it. Of course, I was blowing the money as fast as it was coming in. The job had other perks as well. Dave was always calling me into his office for meetings. Those meetings were simply him pulling a mirror out of desk drawer and the two of us snorting lines to get us through the day.

Dave wasn't as heavyset as his multiple chins made him look. He used to walk around the floor yelling, "maximize the momentum" because for some reason he thought that motivated his employees. He had been divorced a couple of times, due to the fact that "cocaine is my true love". He was prone to panic attacks, which he described as being too sensitive to the universe.

It was while I was doing that job that it occurred to me that I wasn't like everybody else on this planet. I was detached from the rest of the people that surrounded me. I was talking to a lady one day about her credit card bill. "You don't understand sir," she said to me. "My son is going through cancer treatment."

"That's not any of my business," I said.

"Do you understand what I just said to you? My son has stage four Cancer. He is eight years old."

"I understand what you said to me, but it has nothing to do with the fact that you owe $8,764.22 for your Visa bill."

She was silent for a moment. "You are not even treating me like a human being."

I laughed. "You aren't a human being. You are a name on a computer screen with a bunch of numbers next to it. It's my job to make those numbers go to zero."

There were many times when I would just stare out the windows of the skyscraper thinking about the gathering I was at with Miles and Diane. I would think about getting high on the deck with Leno in San Diego, and what he told me about how everything is like a screen on a door and how there were dead zones where certain souls shouldn't go. I tried not to think about Angela and the dead baby, but sometimes I just couldn't help it. I didn't want to have to admit that I didn't have pangs of jealousy for that kid. He was lucky enough to have not had to live through this fucked up world.

On my first night working for the bank, Angela met me in one of my Terminal dreams. This time, the place was more crowded than I had ever seen it. The people walked faster than they had in all of my previous visits. I saw Angela from a distance and in an instant, she was face to face with me. She looked horrible. It was as if she had aged decades from the night, I found her on the bathroom floor.

Her skin had very little color to it, and her lips had a light hue of blue. She was wearing a see-through night gown, still showing off her tits. The night gown was supposed to be white, but had stained to a light yellow, and I noticed that there was dried blood on the inside of her legs. Her breath smelled rotten.

She grabbed me by the hand and guided me to sit next to her on one of the long black benches. Her vacant eyes looked at me as she asked, "Do you know how fake everything is? Do you realize that this is all just an illusion?"

"Of course it's an illusion," I said. "I'm in the middle of a dream. I know this isn't real at all. It's not supposed to be."

My words enraged her. She slapped me. "You stupid mother fucker. Don't you see what is happening all around you?"

"What do you mean Angela?"

"What the fuck is wrong with you?", she screamed. "Look around you. This is no fucking dream. You come from a world that is the goddamn dream. This place is the abyss. This is the place that takes you to somewhere real, but you're too fucking dumb to realize it."

She stood up from the bench and started to walk away, but changed her mind and came back and stood in front of me. "If this is a dream, wake the fuck up, and when you do, you'll be back where you came from and hopefully realize that you need to wake the fuck up there too."

++   ++   ++

There is something about making a lot of money that becomes addicting. I never thought that I would be that guy, but addiction is a personality trait. I was addicted to a lot of things, but never thought of it in those terms. I barely cared about money in my younger years, but with middle age approaching, the pursuit of it became the equivalent of how I felt about cocaine and alcohol. Through the process, I matured to the point where I wasn't looking in my wallet to gauge my net worth. Dave had told me that he would help me do some investing. I started getting envelopes in the mail telling me what I was worth. I actually found myself paying attention to what was happening in the stock market.

Dave was fired from the bank after he got too high and left a mirror of lines on his desk after he going home for the day. After that, I decided to go to work for an even bigger bank. This one had its headquarters on Wall Street. I had been offered a management position, and the money was triple what I had been making at the other bank. There was a lot more stress, but I didn't care once payday came around. The new company had a retirement plan, so I started getting even more envelopes in the mail telling me what I was worth as a human being.

Down in the smoking area of the parking garage, I slowly became friends with a woman named Jacklyn. She was a high-level executive at the bank and she was like no other woman that I had ever met before. She was so focused and driven. She was always impeccably dressed, very sexy as well. She was that unique blend of beauty, brains and power. She was originally from Manhattan and what you would probably describe as a yuppie.

We started going to happy hours at the bar across the street on Fridays. After a couple of months, I'd go home with her and stay for the weekend. She lived alone in a huge house in a very affluent part of town. The place was always perfectly clean and decorated with very expensive furniture. She loved to point at her possessions and tell you how much they cost. She had hired a famous interior decorator to do the place, and it looked great. Most of the art that hung on her walls were original pieces.

I slowly got ingrained into Jaclyn's world of material possessions to the point that I was rarely going home. I eventually just moved in with her. She made it perfectly clear to me that if we were going to be a couple, I was going to have to make some changes. There was no way she was going to be seen with some guy who purchased his suits off of the rack. She took me to a tailor, and the designer suits that I had purchased fit me perfectly.

Also, even though it was a classic car, Jacklyn wasn't going to have an old Datsun 240Z sitting in her driveway. I protested a bit because I really loved that car. I had taken care of it pretty well, but my protests fell on deaf ears. She convinced me that a member of upper management would look so much better tooling around in a brand-new Mercedes. I was so caught up in her way of thinking that it never occurred to me to ask, "Look better to who?"

Life with Jacklyn was all about acquiring things. It was a cycle of working needlessly long hours to get money that we would go spend when we weren't working. Our conversations became about work and shopping. It was nothing for us to go to the mall and drop $5000. Jaclyn bought a single purse one day that cost $3000. She didn't even look at the price tag on a pair of shoes, if she liked them, she was going to buy them no matter what they cost. I started collecting leather jackets for some reason, though I rarely wore them. I had ties that cost $500 and belts that were almost $200.

There would be times that I would sit in my office and try to pinpoint exactly what kind of relationship Jaclyn and I were having. We considered ourselves to be a romantic couple, but we really weren't. We didn't have sex all that often, and when we did it was very vanilla. She was more turned on by me handing a credit card to someone than to have me touch her. The closest I came to defining our relationship is that you were business partners with benefits.

Jacklyn had never liked me doing cocaine, even though she was eating Xanax like tic-tac's. That didn't stop me from doing it, I just became more covert about it. When we went out, it was only to high end restaurants so she could see and be seen. She might have a glass of wine, and would often give me the evil eye if I had more than two drinks. It was while I was eating a filet mignon that it occurred to me how bored I was. The excitement of spending money had worn thin. Jacklyn asked me what was wrong, I just said that I was tired.

Jaclyn came home one day very excited. She grabbed me by the hand, "you need to come outside with me." When we got outside, she pointed to a new Porsche in the driveway. "What do you think?"

"It's nice."

"It's my way of congratulating myself."

"Oh yeah?"

"You are now lovers with newest senior vice president."

"Well deserved. I don't know what to say."

"What you need to say," she said, "is that you promise to start working a lot harder".

"Why is that?"

"You need to get a promotion. This relationship is going to work if we aren't on equal levels in our careers."

I literally laughed out loud thinking that she was joking, but when I looked at her face, I knew that she was dead serious. "That's fucked up," I said.

"I didn't mean it to come out that way. Hey, go get dressed, we'll take a spin and go have some dinner."

We drove the Porsche up into the foothills then found a sushi place in the city for dinner. It was still early when we decided to go to the art district. Many of the galleries would be opening new shows that night, and Jacklyn wanted a new piece for the living room. At the third place we went into, she found an oil on stainless steel painting that she really liked. "It's kind of cheesy," I said.

"It will match the rest of the colors in the room."

"I'm not sure that's really the point of art."

That irritated her. "Why don't you go walk around while I finish the deal and arrange for delivery."

As I walked past the window of one gallery, a painting caught my eye. It was bold and bright, but at the same time dark and disturbing. I went in and stared at it. It was an abstract piece, but I saw images on the canvass. It struck me as some type of battle scene. It made me think of the slaughter at the gallery so many years earlier. This gallery was different from the others. There were actually artists working while the show was going on.

I noticed a girl painting in the corner, and I knew right away that she was the artist who had done the piece that I was admiring. She was beautiful. The way that she moved as she painted could best be described as liquid. It was like the brush in her hand was channeling itself, and she flowed with what appeared to be very little effort. I watched her for a while. Not only was she creating art, she was her own work of performance art.

I cautiously approached her. I didn't want to disturb her as she worked. As I got closer, my skin started to buzz. I could feel her aura of energy or whatever you want to call it.

"Excuse me," I said. "Did you happen to do that painting up by the door?"

She stopped what she was doing. She looked me up and down. She had beautiful eyes, but there was disdain in them probably because of the designer suit and $500 shoes.

"Yeah." Then she went back to what she was doing.

"I really like it," I said.

She flashed me a half-hearted smile, "my business cards are up front. It has my web page on it."

I grabbed one of her business cards. Her name was Angelica. For some reason, it gave me shivers when I thought about how close her name was to Angela's. As I walked out the door, I caught a reflection of myself in the glass. I couldn't believe what I was looking at. "A suit and a tie on a Friday night?", I said out loud to myself. The clothes that I was wearing had cost me more than $3000, but I may have well been dressed in rags the way I felt about myself at that moment.

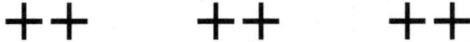

As I sat in the chair with a beer looking at the girl sleeping on my mattress, she would randomly say the word "shadow" as well some other things that I couldn't understand. Some of it sounded like it was in a foreign language. I think she might have even said some phrases in Latin, but I couldn't be sure. I didn't respond to anything she said, because I didn't want to disturb her.

I was almost delirious from the coke, beer, and lack of sleep when the girl said, "there's a dead baby on the floor". My heart started pounding. It occurred to me that this lovely young beauty was merely talking in her sleep. Maybe she wasn't even sleeping at all, but in some other state of altered consciousness.

"The baby on the floor is covered in blood," she said.

I wanted to grab her and wake her up and ask what she was talking about, but I already knew. She wasn't merely talking in her sleep. I could feel that she was in my mind. Maybe her words wouldn't have been audible to another person. I was hearing her thoughts as she explored my soul.

"It's good thing about the baby," she said. "It was never supposed to be here. It was just lost, but he found the way back.

"I know," I said.

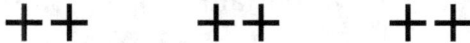

The next morning, I went into the back of the closet and pulled out the duffel bag of clothes that I had before Jaclyn started dressing me. I put on a tank top, a pair of cotton gym shorts and some sandals. When I went downstairs, she stared at me the way a teacher would stare at a student who had just done something wrong.

"What are your plans for the day?" she asked.

"I'm going to the bar as soon as it opens, and drink all day."

"Is there something that's a matter?"

"Everything is the matter. I'm tired of living like this."

"What the hell are you talking about? We have a perfect life. This is almost everything we have ever wanted".

"It's a fucking façade Jacklyn. It isn't real".

"I don't like this side of you."

"I don't give a fuck what you like. This is who I am."

"We are very important people," she said.

"No were not. We don't do anything. We move other people's money around electronically and then take our little cut. We contribute nothing to society. It's not even real money. It's just numbers. We like to pretend that it's money that were talking about, but it's just numbers that don't mean shit."

"Look around you Vincent…"

"Fuck you Jacklyn. We're nothing more than mannequins. We wear clothes for other people to admire. I'm tired of being part of a show. I want to feel alive again."

"Maybe you should go to a doctor Vincent. There might be some medication that could help you."

"Once I get to the bar, I'll have plenty of medication that will help me."

The following Monday morning, I walked into work with a box and cleaned my office out. I sent human resources an email of my resignation and left. The next stop was the bank, where I withdrew everything that I had in cash. It wasn't as much as I had expected, but I hadn't really been keeping track of my expenses lately. I drove to my storage unit, parked the Mercedes in it and drove away in the 240Z. I went back to Jacklyn's and packed up only the stuff that I had when I arrived. I would leave it up to her to deal with all of the shit I had bought since I lived there.

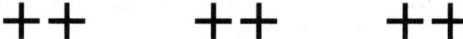

As I drove, with no particular place in mind, I started thinking about Angelica, the artist I had met a few nights earlier. I decided that I needed to see her again. I wanted to show her that I wasn't really the tool that she had seen in a shirt and tie. I drove to the gallery, but it wasn't open. In fact, the only time that it was open was on the weekends. I walked up and down the street looking in the windows. I came across a sign in one of the windows that had studio space for rent.

The place came furnished with a bed, a table and chair, and a small kitchen. It was a big difference from Jacklyn's place, but it was all that I needed. I found a bar down the street and went in for a few drinks. As I sat there alone drinking, I couldn't help but wonder if I had done the right thing. I had it made, I was making good money, and I had everything that I wanted and even more that I didn't want. Still, it felt right. There was something about the whole move that made me feel excited. It had been a long time since I had woken up in the morning and been eager to see what the day brings.

It was going to be a long time before I had to worry about money. I had plenty of cash, and if things got rough, I could sell the Mercedes. I figured that I could probably go a few years without needing a job. I was still getting envelopes telling me what I was worth. I decided that since I was living in an art district that I should try to do something creative. I went and bought a computer in case I had a story that was worth writing. I got some canvasses, oil paints, and other supplies. Maybe I had some talents that I didn't know about.

Almost every day I walked by the gallery where I had seen Angelica, but she was never there. When I went there on a Friday, the painting that I had enjoyed so much was gone, replaced by a different artist's work. There was somebody else painting in the corner where I had seen her. When I walked out of the place, I noticed that her business cards were no longer there.

I became a frequent visitor to all of the galleries in the area hoping to see Angelica again. I would ask about her, and came across people that knew her, but they had no idea where she might be. I even drove to some of the other art districts in the city, but I never came across her or any paintings that looked like they might have been hers. I had run out of options. There was nowhere else to look.

It was the first day of summer, and I decided to mark the occasion by going to the bar. I was sitting out on the patio, smoking cigarettes, drinking beer, and asking myself what it was that I was going to do with the rest of my life. I watched as the sky grew darker as a coming storm started to gather strength. When it started raining, I thought about going inside, but decided instead to move to a table that had an umbrella over it. I was in awe of the lightening show that was going on around me.

"Is it okay if I sit here while I have cigarette?", a woman's voice asked from behind me.

"Yes," I said without even looking.

I couldn't believe it when Angelica sat down across me. She was even more beautiful than I remember her. It became obvious that she had no memory of me at all. I thought about reminding her, but I didn't want her to think of me as that guy in the designer suit. The rain became torrential, and the wind picked up. It was getting hard to stay dry even under the umbrella.

"Can I buy you a drink inside?" I asked. She looked at me suspiciously but still said yes.

We made small talk about the weather and the people at the bar. "What do you do for a living?" I asked, fully expecting her to tell me that she was an artist.

"I'm a bartender at a place a few blocks from here."

We kept making small talk about mundane bullshit, and as we talked, I realized that the eyes I had become so enamored with the first time that I met her were the gateway to something darker. You could tell that those eyes had seen a lot, they portrayed a person that had been hardened by life but somehow survived. Without a word, her eyes communicated that there wasn't a whole lot in this world that Angelica gave a fuck about.

"We need to do some shots", she said. "I'm ready to get fucked up."

"What do you want?"

"I don't know. Fireball or Jägermeister."

I told the bartender to get us two Fireballs. The more we drank, the looser and louder Angelica became. She started dancing to the music on the Jukebox. As she moved, it reminded me of the time that I was watching her paint. She had that same flow, her dancing was effortless, it was as if the music didn't even matter. She just kept dancing and doing shots until the place closed down.

"If you want to keep the party going," I said to her, "I don't live too far away".

"I guess. There's no way that either of us can drive."

"I'll call a cab if you want."

"Let's just walk to your place. We'll have a couple of more drinks, then I'll call for a ride home."

We did some more shots when we got back to my place and smoked a bowl. "Instead of calling for a ride," I said, "you can just stay here. I promise to be a complete gentleman".

"I don't think I want you to be a gentleman". She pulled me close and kissed me hard and deep. "Fuck that gentleman bullshit. Just fuck me. Give me everything you've got."

I was more than obliged. She had a petite hard body with small tits and pierced nipples. She had a few sporadic tattoos. For the next two hours we had sex that could only be described as "animalistic". As I grinded between her legs, she dug her fingernails into me leaving scratches the length of my back. She bit my nipples so hard that I thought for sure that I was bleeding. Her pussy was tight and a perfect fit for my dick. There was something about Angelica. I felt connected to her in a way that I had never felt with anybody else.

The next morning, we were both extremely hungover. We decided to drive somewhere up in the mountains and get some breakfast. We didn't talk much during the drive, probably because both of our heads were screaming in agony. It wasn't until we got some food in our stomach that we started talking about the previous night.

"I have a confession to make," she said.

"What?"

"I don't know your name."

"It's Vincent. Now that I think about it, I don't think the subject ever came up."

"I'm Angelica".

"I have a confession to make too."

"Don't tell me your married, or have a girlfriend."

I laughed, "no that's not what it is at all. I know who you are. I watched you paint one night. I grabbed one of your business cards from the gallery".

"I hope that you're not offended, but I don't remember that at all. I get into a zone when I paint. It's like this world doesn't exist at all. It's like I'm in a different universe or something".

"I'm not offended. I'm grateful. There was something about watching you paint that night that inspired me to quit my job, get out of a boring relationship, and start living again."

The look on her face was priceless. "Thanks. I guess."

"How long have you been painting?" I asked.

"I don't know, a year or so."

"Fuck off. I saw one of your paintings. It was awesome. The whole reason I walked into the gallery."

"I know the one you're talking about. I didn't think it was that good. I just like painting. It's like therapy for me and a whole lot fucking cheaper than a psychiatrist."

"Why didn't you start painting earlier in life?"

"That's a long, sordid story Vincent. It's just something that I will have to tell you later. We haven't even known each other a full day. I don't want to scare you away that fast".

"Fair enough. I don't think that you could scare me away, but I'm happy that you feel that way, because I really would like to see you again."

I drove her to her house, and she got out of the car, she said, "I have one more confession to make."

"Okay."

"I have a boyfriend."

"That doesn't bother me."

She smiled, and gave me a kiss. "You should come into my work. I'll buy you a few drinks."

I started going to Angelica's bar for a few beers every night that she worked. I didn't pursue her as much as I would have liked to because of the boyfriend situation but eventually that corrected itself and he just disappeared. After a few weeks, she would just walk to my place after she got off of work and just sleep there. I gave her a key so that she could come and go as she wanted. Before long, she wasn't even going to her own house except to get some different clothes. We were spending every moment that we could together.

Angelica was a private person. She was very guarded about who she let into her inner circle. She slowly told me what she had been through over the course of her life. She had a daughter that lived out of state with whom she had very little contact. She was trying to reestablish a relationship with her after not seeing her for most of her childhood. It was a slow process, but Angelica seemed to think that it was going well.

The reason that Angelica wasn't in her daughter's life was because she had had a major drug problem for most of her life. She started selling cocaine when she was sixteen working as cocktail waitress at a strip club. When she moved to Colorado, she hooked up with a guy that was a big meth user. After a while, the drug made them so paranoid that they moved out of an apartment and into a storage unit because they couldn't stand the windows. She said that at some point he told her that she couldn't leave. It was too dangerous. She said that the meth made her so horny that she spent the next year and a half locked up in the storage unit masturbating all day. All they did when he was around was smoke meth and fuck. One day he was so high, he forgot to paddle lock on the unit after he left and she hadn't smoked meth since.

One morning I woke up early for no apparent reason. I made myself a cup of coffee, sat at the table and just watched Angelica sleep. I could feel myself smile. I felt good. I actually felt happy. I thought to myself, this is what my life is supposed to be. I had found my purpose, and she was sleeping in my bed. I realized how totally in love I was with Angelica.

That afternoon we walked out of the Justice of the Peace's office as husband and wife. Angelica wanted to get a place that we could call our own. We found a spacious three-room cabin in the mountains that overlooked Denver. We turned one room into a studio where we could paint or create whatever we wanted. The first two years of our marriage was filled with love, peace and contentment, except for a few alcohol-fueled arguments. Angelica could be a mean drunk. I had never felt like that in my entire life.

We would drive out of state a couple of times a year to see Angelica's daughter. Slowly that relationship began to mend after years of neglect. On the night of our third anniversary, my wife got a call from her daughter to inform her that she was going to be a grandma. She was smiling as tears ran down her face, "I'm too young to be a grandma".

When her daughter was almost due to give birth, Angelica was going to go stay with her until the baby came. Angelica hadn't been feeling well for about a month, and she thought that maybe going home and helping with the baby might make her feel better. I decided that while she was gone, I was going to take a road trip.

"Where are you going to go?" Angelica asked.

"I'll know when I get there."

"Sounds fun."

"Maybe Mexico."

++   ++   ++

The night before we each went on our trips, I had one of my Terminal dreams. As I walked through the place, I noticed that it was brighter than it had been on any of my previous experiences. It was also much noisier. I felt a tap on my shoulder. I turned around and was face to face with Miles.

"It's good to see you again," I said.

"There is something I need to tell you." His words were stern. He wasn't there for a reunion. "I wish that I would have told you earlier."

"What is it?"

"It's about Anima"

"You knew her?" I was surprised. I don't recall ever mentioning her to him.

"It's not really important how I knew her, besides we don't have a lot of time."

"Say what you have to say Miles"

"Anima was raped when she was younger. It was a brutal rape by a gang of men who grabbed her off the street. She spent months in the hospital recovering."

"Why did you need to tell me this?

"She had to have a hysterectomy. She would never be able to have children of her own."

"I'll ask you again Miles. Why are you telling me this?"

"You need to know."

"Why?"

"You just do."

After my encounter with Miles, I changed my mind about going to Mexico. I decided that I was going to recreate the travels that I had done when I was younger. I kissed Angelica goodbye and she headed east and I headed west. As I drove towards Utah, I thought about my wife and was a little bit worried. She hadn't been looking good lately. She had lost weight that she never had to lose in the first place and was always complaining that she didn't have any energy. She promised me that she would go to a doctor when she got back.

Late in the afternoon I got to the campground at Lake Powell where I had met Miles decades earlier. The sun was brutal. It was well over 100 degrees. I went for a swim to cool off. I had brought my painting supplies with me and I spent a couple of days by the water using acrylic paint to recreate the beautiful scenery that surrounded me. The canyon walls seemed so haunting that I wanted to capture them. There were one or two paintings that I really liked, and there were a few others that looked very amateurish. I ended up painting over them.

Even before I started driving, I debated whether I wanted to go to the site where the gathering of like minds had been. After a few days of soaking up the sun in Utah, I decided that I needed to see that place again. The big question was whether I would be able to find it. I started heading that way at sunrise one morning. I wasn't in a hurry, so I planned on being there in a couple of days.

My worries about finding the place were completely unfounded. I drove right to it. As I drove down the dirt road, I started noticing little plumes of smoke rising into the air. It looked like there were some people camping there. As the valley came into view, I saw that there were hundreds of people there. It felt like a dream. It looked like the exact same gathering I had been to years earlier. I got out of the car and looked around. Had it not been for the newer models of vehicles I would have thought that I was in some type of time warp. Even some of the people looked familiar.

A young guy with a beard came over and welcomed me.

"You can pitch a tent wherever you find an open space," he said. "You're free to stay as long as you want".

"What type of gathering is this?"

"It's just a group of people who all come together because they feel connected in some way".

I thought about telling him that I had been here years before and about what had happened, but decided against it. I just thanked him.

I looked at the passage through the trees where Miles had walked into the first time I was there. I walked into it and found the trail. About a half mile into the hike, I came to a rocky outcrop that overlooked the valley where everybody else was. I had nothing better to do, so after a couple of trips back and forth to the car, I had my tent set up, a cooler full of beer, and a fire made. My painting supplies were in the tent if the mood struck me.

I spent the night alone on the outcrop looking out over the activity below me, drinking beer in the flicker of the campfire. I wondered if any of those people down there had any idea what had happened here. I thought about the possibility of being slaughtered, but dismissed the notion. It couldn't happen again. I asked myself how it was that a group of people who didn't know each gathered at the same place on two occasions. Maybe there were more than two occasions, maybe these gatherings were happening on a continual basis.

The next day I woke up late in the morning, I could hear music. I looked down at the people gathered below me. They had all converged around five guys playing instruments and singing. I was too far away to make out the lyrics. I pulled out a canvas and started painting what I was seeing before me. In about two hours, I had created a piece that I thought was one of the best things that I had ever done. It spoke to me. It made me think of Diane.

The next morning, I decided that I needed to get going. It seemed only natural to leave the gathering and drive to the beach that Diane and I had once driven to. I got to the coast a couple of days later just as the sun was setting. I sat on a cliff and stared out over the water. Just as was about to slip below the horizon creating night, I saw a figure emerge from the rocks below me. I watched as the figure casually walked into the waves. The figure never looked back, it just walked forward until it dropped below the surface. Instead of camping there that night, I just went and found a hotel room.

The next morning, Angela called me to tell me that the baby had been born. It was a healthy baby boy; the delivery had gone smoothly and her daughter was fine.

"How are you feeling?" I asked.

"I'm exhausted. I always feel that way anymore. I have been having these weird pains in my stomach."

"You better go to a doctor".

"I'll go when I get back".

"When's that going to be?"

"Probably two or three weeks."

"Okay. Let me know when you are on your way, and I'll start heading that direction too."

I was in no rush, so I took my time driving south down the California coast. I would only drive an hour or two each day, if I drove at all, then I would camp on the beach, or find a hotel room that over looked the ocean. I did a few more paintings, and took some nice photos. I kept telling myself how good life was. I had a wife that I loved more than I thought it was possible to love another person. I had very little stress in my life. It was simply a feeling of pure contentment.

I finally found myself in San Diego after about a week and a half. My plan was to stay there until I got a call from Angelica telling me that she was heading home. I could get to Denver in a couple of days. It would take her at least that long to get home. The first thing I did when I got off of Interstate Five was to drive to the house where I had spent all that time living in a closet.

As I turned onto the street, I looked up to the balcony that used to be out of Leno's bedroom. There was somebody up there. The person stood up and watched my car as it approached. As I got closer, I realized it was Leno who was watching me. He had aged very well, he looked almost the same now as he did back then.

"Hello," I yelled to Leno as I got out of the car.

"Who are you?"

"Vincent".

"The Vincent who left with Angela".

"Yes".

"Holy shit. You're still alive?"

I laughed. "Yes".

"I thought you died years ago."

"Where did you hear that?"

He ignored the question. "Come up and have a beer".

I walked into the place, and it was obvious that there had been a party there the night before. Leno was still renting the place out to people, mostly young surfers. Leno hugged me as I walked into his room. "Grab a beer from the cooler and come out on the deck".

"Leno, I can't believe that we are on a deck facing inland when there is a beautiful sunset going on behind us."

"Do you remember the reason for that?"

"I do".

"Well, you missed out on a great sunrise this morning".

He lit a joint. "You look great," I said. "You haven't changed at all."

"You're right. I haven't changed. I've been doing pretty much the same thing every day since you left. But you, on the other hand. I would never have known you if you hadn't told me".

"It's been a wild ride since we last saw each other". I told him about what had happened to Angela. He said that he had heard. I told him all about my life after she died. I told him about Xavier, and Jacklyn, and making all that money. I also told him about Angelica, and how she made me feel so alive.

"It sounds like you really love her".

"I do. She's my world."

"That's great."

We were pretty buzzed by that point. "Leno, why were you so surprised to see me when I pulled up?"

The usual smile that he had on his face disappeared. "Well, Vincent, I was never sure you were alive in the first place".

"Why do you say that?"

He pointed to the screen. "I know I explained to you about how the multiverse is like a screen".

"I remember that".

"I just always assumed that you were one of the souls trapped in a dead zone".

"Maybe".

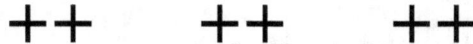

That night I went to the Terminal in my dreams. This time the place was completely deserted. I sat down on one of the black benches and marveled at the emptiness of such a vast place. Although I didn't see anybody else around, I had the feeling that I wasn't alone. I got up and started walking with no idea of where I was going. From a distance, I could see what looked like a black box sitting on the floor.

As I got closer, I realized that it wasn't a black box at all. It was a bassinette with black sheets flowing out of it. When I got close enough and looked inside, I saw that it was the fetus that had been lifeless between Angela's legs.

"I've been waiting for you Vincent," it said with the voice of an old man.

"Hello," I said.

"Do you know who I am?"

"I was your father. Angela was your mother. You both died on the floor of a bathroom in Grand Junction."

He just laughed. "You have no mother fucking clue who I am."

"If you weren't my child, who are you?"

"First of all, asshole, I'm not a child and I never have been. I'm not even a human. I'm a beacon."

"A beacon for what?"

He raised his voice and spoke with a tone of frustration, "goddammit Vincent, everything has been explained to you. You just don't seem to be listening."

"Who is it that I should be listening too?"

"Yourself."

++   ++   ++

I drove back to the cabin in the mountains a day and half before Angelica was supposed to be back. I was excited to see her. I unpacked the car and started to clean the place up. I came across the painting that I had done on the outcropping of rocks overlooking the gathering. I loved what I had created. It made me feel as though I really had the potential to be an artist if I put my mind to it. I decided to hang it on the wall.

When Angelica walked through the door, she didn't look good at all. She had lost even more weight than before she left. I hugged and kissed her as I ran my hands down her body, I could feel her skeleton.

"How do you feel?" I asked.

"I'm okay. I just feel tired".

"Why don't you go lay on the couch for a while. I'll get your bags out of the car, and cook dinner".

As she was eating, she pointed to the painting that I had done and asked me what it was. I described to her where it had come from and how it came to be.

"I really like the artistic quality of it, but it makes me feel bad," she said.

"Why?"

"It reminds of somewhere I was when I was young".

"Where was that?"

"I don't remember. Will you take it down?"

I thought about arguing with her, because I was very proud of the painting, but I just did what she asked me to. I was disappointed and my feelings were hurt, but I took it down and put up a mirror in its place. She got up and wrapped her arms around me. "That is the best painting that you have ever done. Maybe it's just too powerful. I don't like the way that it makes me feel. Uncomfortable. It brings back a lot of bad memories".

"Tell me about them".

"Not tonight".

She was so weak that night that I had to help her to bed. As we lay in bed holding each other, she whispered in my ear, "I'm really worried".

"What are you worried about?"

"There is something really wrong with me. I can feel it".

"Describe it to me".

"I'm getting the feeling that I don't belong in this world anymore".

"Is it something I've done?"

She laughed. "Quit being so egomaniacal. It has nothing to do with you".

We had a good laugh, and fell asleep.

It was right before dawn that I woke up to find Angelica sitting straight up on the edge of the bed. She was shaking, and sweat was running down her face. "What's wrong?"

"Nothing. I just had a dream that really freaked me out".

"It must have been a bad one".

"I'm not even sure if it was a dream. It was like I was somewhere else as this body was sleeping."

I didn't say anything. I had never told Angelica, or anybody else for that matter, about the dreams that I had had my entire life. "It was like I was in some type of bus station, or airport, or something," she said. "There was a girl in it that I had met while I was camping when I was younger. Her name was Diane. In the dream I sat down on a bench and started talking to her. She told me how much fun she had had with me while we were playing in the river at the campsite. There was a voice coming from somewhere in the station calling out for Diane. The voice was telling her that the ocean was waiting for her, whatever that meant. It was fucking weird".

"You should go back to sleep baby. It was just a dream".

Later that same morning, Angelica woke me up. "You need to take me to the emergency room".

"Okay, what's going on?"

"I don't know. We just have to go".

I took her to the hospital, and after an hour and a half wait, they took her into a room. They did all the normal tests, and an x-ray, and an MRI, and after all that the doctor said that he wanted to do even more tests. They took her to a different room, and we waited. After two more hours, the doctor walked in. I could tell by the look on his face that there wasn't going to be anything good to say. He said that they found a problem. Angelica asked what the problem was. The doctor looked at her and then at me. It was a problem that they wouldn't be able to correct. Angelica asked if there was anybody who would be able to correct the problem. He didn't respond vocally. He just shook his head.

They admitted her into the hospital. I slept in a chair as Angelica had various tubes and needles inserted into her. When I woke up, I went over to ask her how she was. She didn't respond. I shook her shoulder lightly, but she still didn't stir. I looked up at the vital sign monitor. She was still alive. I kept trying to nudge her awake, but she wasn't responding.

The doctor walked into the room and saw what I was trying to do. He put his arm around me, and told me what was going to happen. Angelica was dead before the sun went down.

After Angelica died, I got rid of everything that I owned. If it wasn't going to fit in the car, I wasn't going to need it. I just roamed around the country. Most of the time I didn't even know where I was. I was driving aimlessly. I wasn't paying attention to the scenery around me. If the road came to a dead end, I flipped a coin to see if I was going to turn right.

One night, in a motel room in God knows where, I was had one of my Terminal dreams. This time the place was dark. I couldn't see the faces of the people who passed by me. I was the only one walking in the direction that I was going. All of the faceless figures were walking the direction that I had just come from. They would brush past me without saying a word. I kept walking until there was only one figure in front of me.

"Hello Vitorum," the faceless figure said to me. It was the voice of an elderly lady. It was the woman who had raised me, Anima.

"Hello."

"I spoke to Miles."

"How do you know Miles?" I asked.

"We've known each other forever." She said it in such a dismissive way, I knew she was telling the truth. "What he told you when you met him here was only partially true."

"I don't feel like Miles has ever lied to me before," I told her.

"He didn't really lie to you, he just didn't tell you the truth. It was true that the doctors told me that I wouldn't be able to have children after what that group of men did to me, and back in those days a decent man didn't want a woman who couldn't bare him children."

"That's what I've heard," I said.

"I started hanging out with men who weren't decent. One thing led to another and somehow, somewhere along the line I became a prostitute. It turns out the doctors were wrong. I was terrified to find out that I was pregnant. I wanted so badly to have an abortion, but in a small town in 1965 that wasn't an option."

"What happened to the baby," I asked, but I wasn't really sure that I wanted to hear the answer.

"It was you."

"Why didn't you tell me?"

"I didn't want you to get attached to me. I was a prostitute, who knew what was going to happen. Xavier was born a few years later."

"You don't have to worry we didn't get attached to you."

"I know," she said. "I thought that was something that you needed to know. She walked past me and followed the faceless figures marching in the opposite direction of the Terminal.

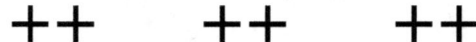

The night before I brought the girl home from the bar, I made another journey to the Terminal in my dreams. But this time it really wasn't the Terminal. Well, it was, but this time there is no floor. It was just a huge river and I am floating along in it. I feel the current starting to get stronger, it goes from a peaceful flow to raging whitewater in just a few moments. I get violently sucked down into an undercurrent. I struggle to get back to the surface, but am just continuously beaten down. I get tired of fighting the water and make peace with the fact that this is where my time comes to an end. I can feel the water seeping into my lungs. I am dying and am overwhelmed with a sense of contentment. I feel my lips being molded into a smile. In that moment of perfect stillness, I find myself back on the surface of the water. The river is a peaceful flow again. I open my eyes and see bright lights. I hear the wail of a newborn baby.

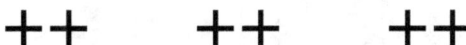

I was staring out the window thinking about the girl who talked about the dead baby on the floor. The image of that night in bathroom with Angela so many years earlier stuck in my head. I glanced over at the girl. She was staring at me.

"You awake?" I asked.

"Always," she said.

I didn't say anything.

"Is it time Vincent?"

"Time for what?"

"You know exactly what I'm talking about." She got up off the bed and stood naked in front of me. She picked up the gun and looked at it, then sat it back down. "It's time for you to come home. It's taken a very long time for me to find you. You have been very lost."

"I don't have a home," I told her.

"Not at this intersection you don't."

"What do you mean?"

"You're in a dead zone Vincent. Your soul is trapped here. Don't you realize that you only think you are having a life here. It's not real. Everything is an illusion. Everywhere else, in all of the other billions of universes, your soul thrives. You are a man of stature and respect. Here, you are but a ghost."

"What is your name?" I asked her.

She smiled at me, then walked over to the dark part of the room where I could only make out her silhouette.

"Don't you recognize me Vincent? I am Anima. I am Diane, I walked into the ocean hoping you would follow me."

"I didn't know."

"I am Angela. When I was Angelica, I was sure that I was going to get you out of this place, but things didn't go as I had planned."

"Were you Jaclyn too?"

She laughed out loud and walked back over to me. "No, Jacklyn is just like you. A baby that should have been still born, but through your own stubbornness you survived. I would suspect that there is a shadow out there looking for her if they haven't found her already."

"Are you a shadow?"

She ignored the question. "It's time Vincent."

"Okay."

I snorted the last line of cocaine and put the gun to my head.